CRUNCH

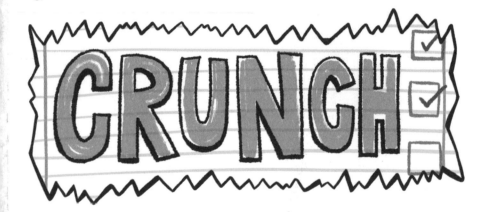

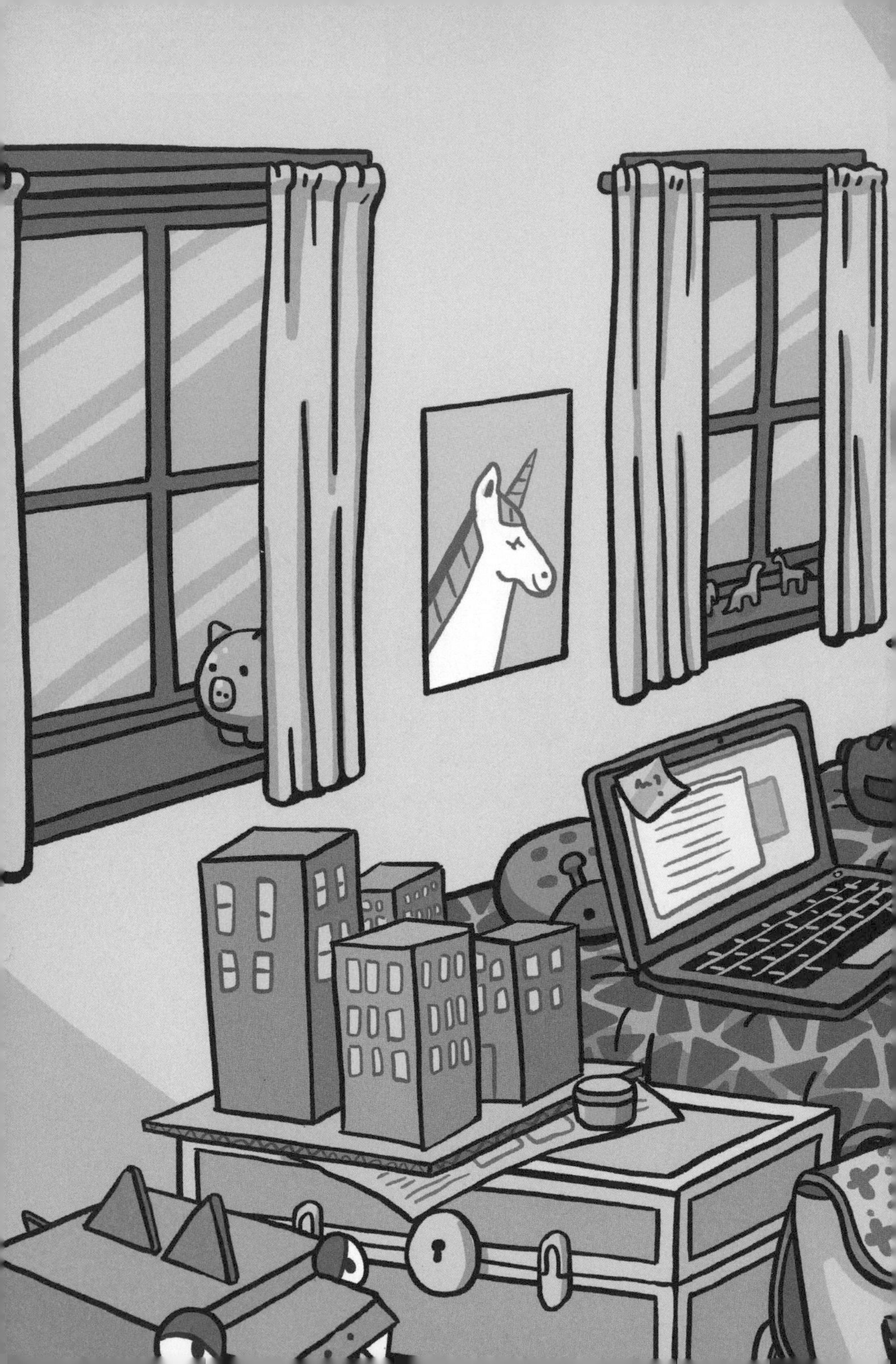

CRUNCH

BY KAYLA MILLER

CLARION BOOKS
IMPRINTS OF HARPERCOLLINSPUBLISHERS

HARPER
alley

FOR THOSE OF US WHO NEED A BREAK. —KM

COLOR BY JESS LOME
LETTERING BY LOR PRESCOTT

Clarion Books is an imprint of HarperCollins Publishers.
HarperAlley is an imprint of HarperCollins Publishers.

Crunch

ISBN 978-0-35-841421-6 hardcover
ISBN 978-0-35-839368-9 paperback

The artist used Photoshop to create
the digital illustrations for this book.
Typography by Stephanie Hays
22 23 24 25 26 GPS 10 9 8 7 6 5 4 3 2 1
First Edition

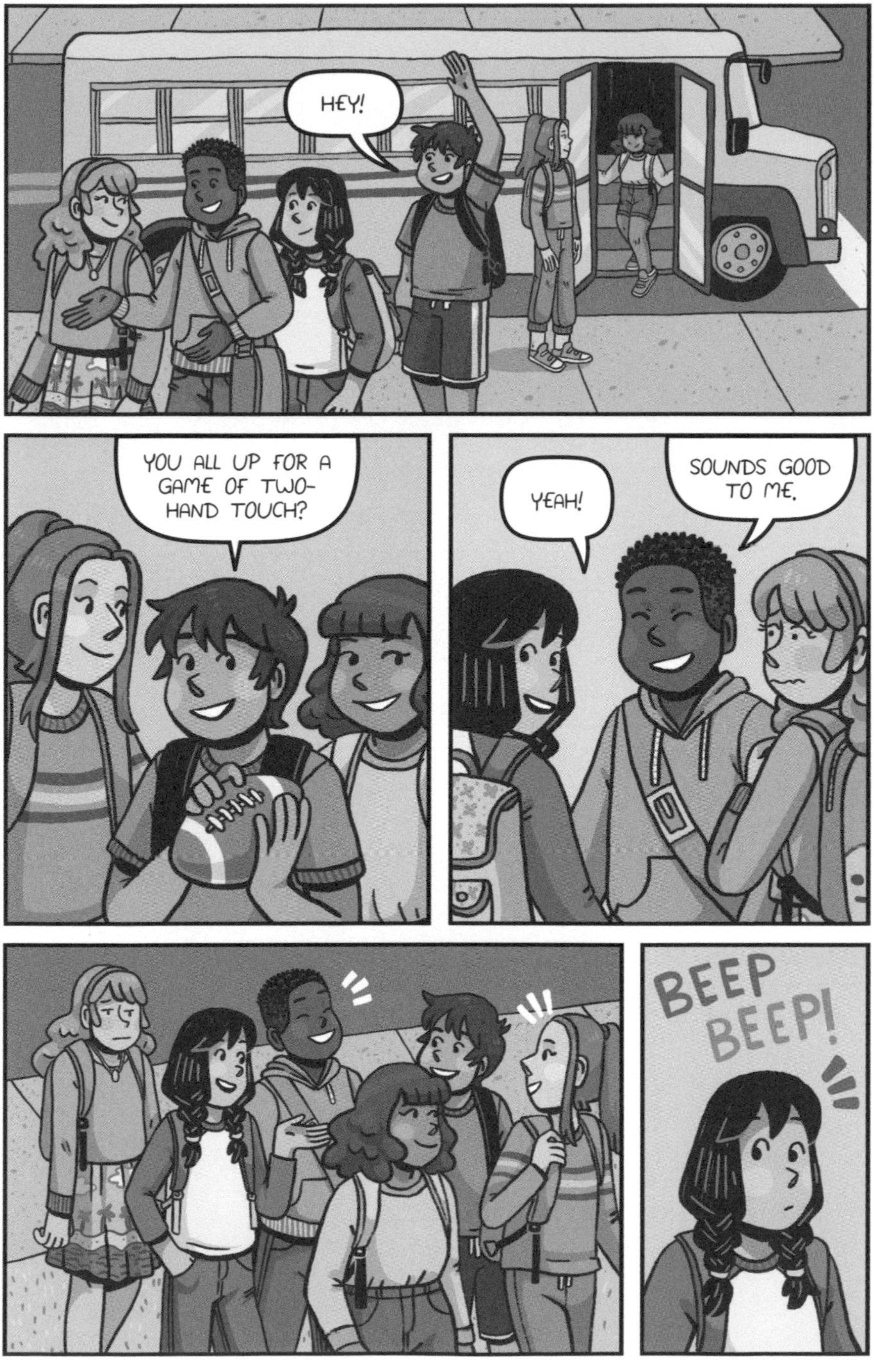
HEY!
YOU ALL UP FOR A GAME OF TWO-HAND TOUCH?
YEAH!
SOUNDS GOOD TO ME.
BEEP BEEP!

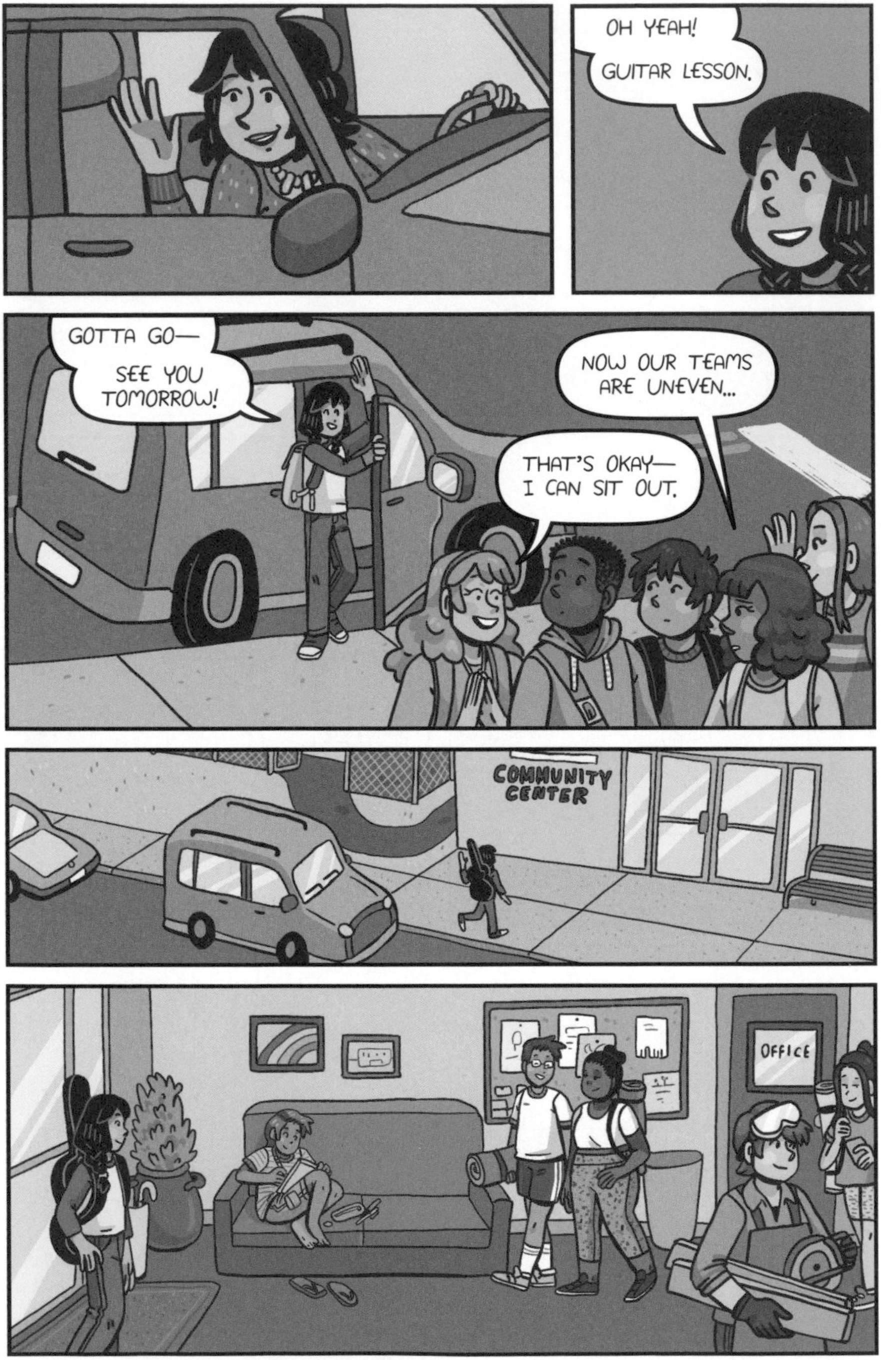
OH YEAH!
GUITAR LESSON.
GOTTA GO—
SEE YOU TOMORROW!
NOW OUR TEAMS ARE UNEVEN...
THAT'S OKAY— I CAN SIT OUT.
COMMUNITY CENTER
OFFICE

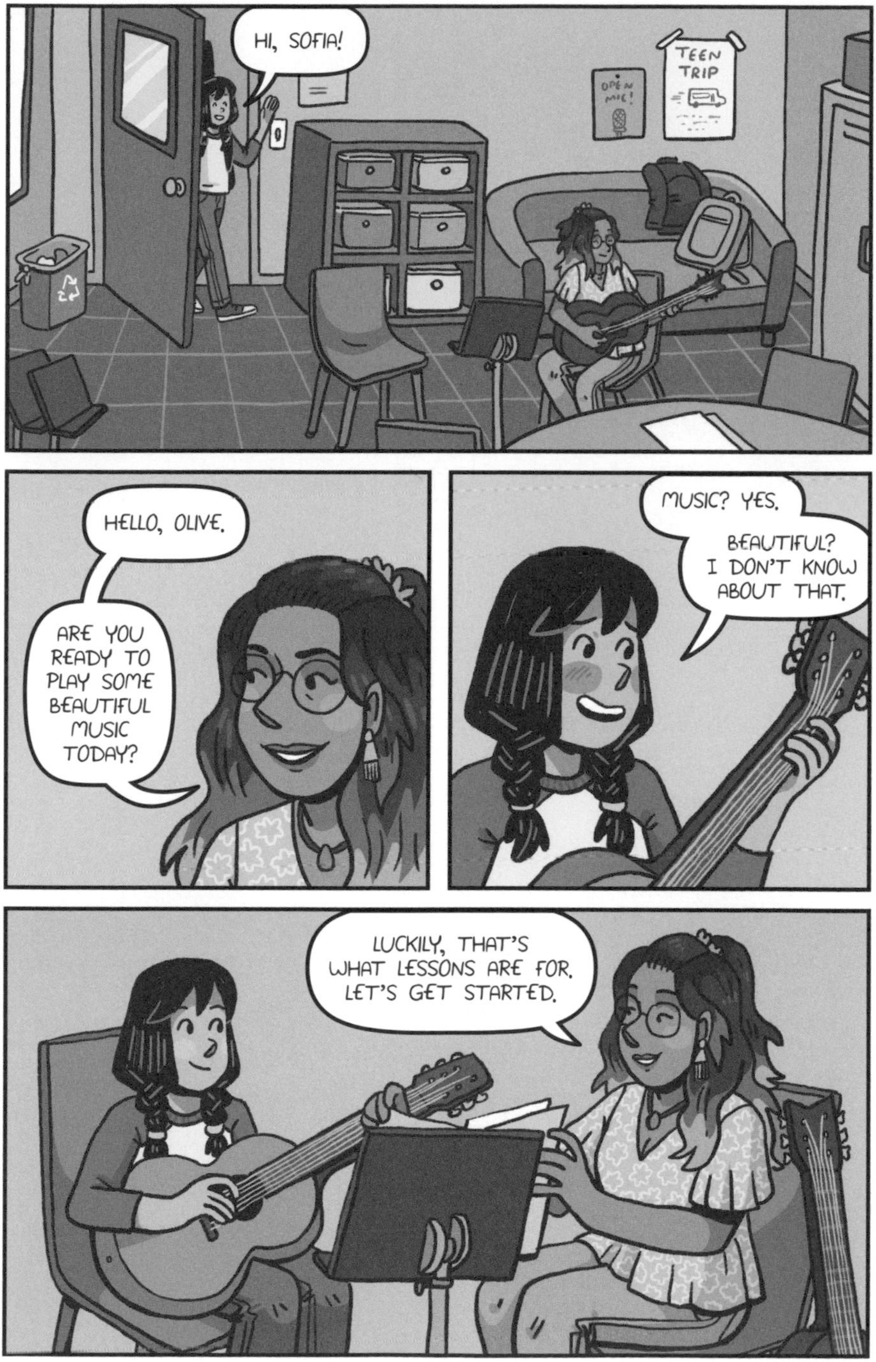
HI, SOFIA!
TEEN TRIP
OPEN MIC!
HELLO, OLIVE.
ARE YOU READY TO PLAY SOME BEAUTIFUL MUSIC TODAY?
MUSIC? YES.
BEAUTIFUL? I DON'T KNOW ABOUT THAT.
LUCKILY, THAT'S WHAT LESSONS ARE FOR. LET'S GET STARTED.

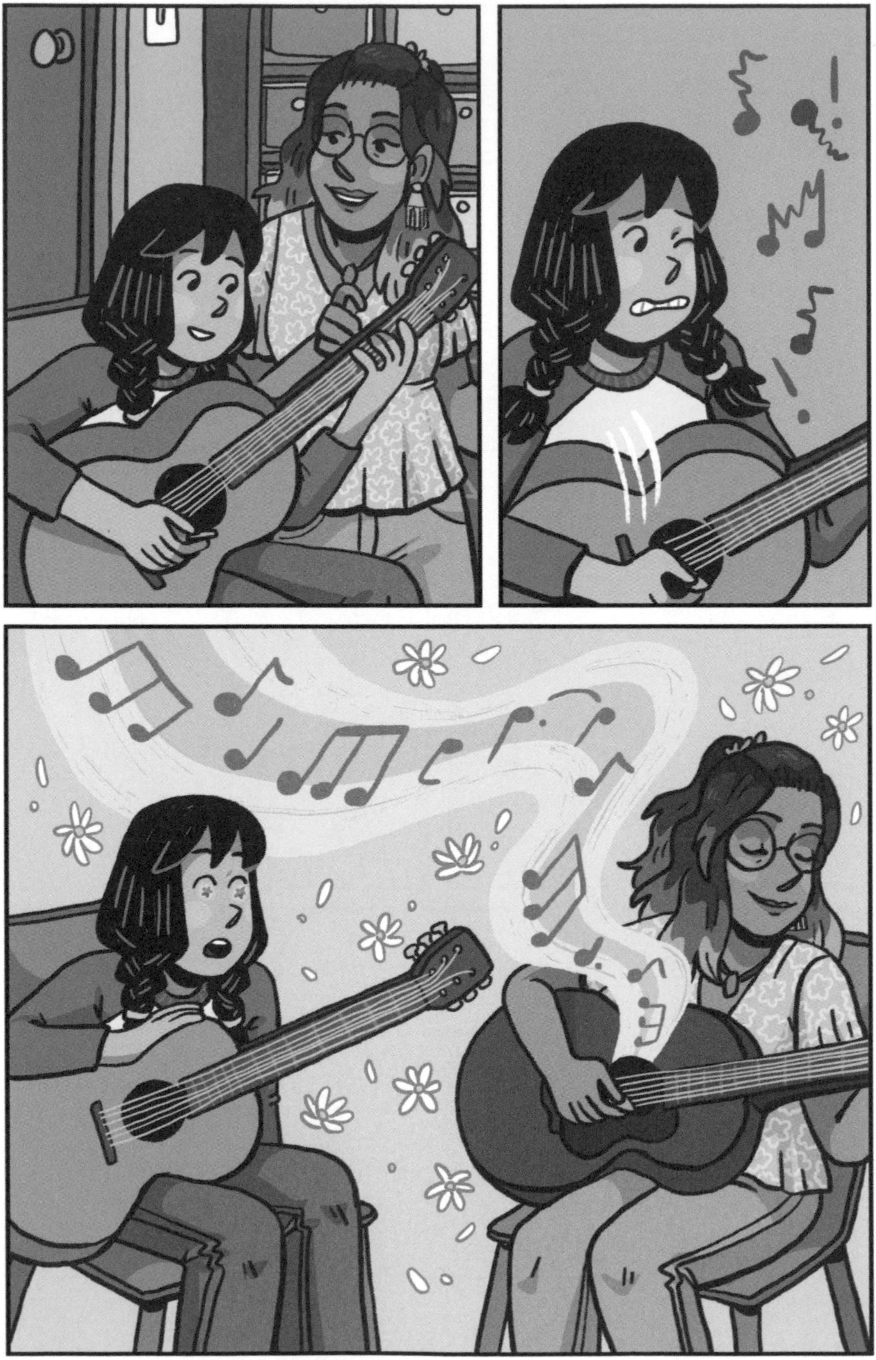

YOU DID A GREAT JOB TODAY!

YOU HAVE A FUNNY DEFINITION OF "GREAT."

DON'T BE SO HARD ON YOURSELF. YOU'RE JUST STARTING OUT...AND FOR A BEGINNER, YOU'RE DOING REALLY WELL.

JUST KEEP UP WITH YOUR PRACTICING. THREE HOURS A WEEK, REMEMBER?

YOU GOT IT, TEACH.

HEY, SUGAR.
READY TO
HEAD OUT?

YEAH,
ONE SEC.

RIP!

AND WE NAMED THEM "NOODLE" BECAUSE THEY LOOKED LIKE A GREEN ELBOW NOODLE, BUT THEN WE CHANGED THEIR NAME TO "SOUP" BECAUSE MISS KELLY TOLD US TH... ...ERPILLARS TURN INTO ...RE INSIDE THEIR C... ...KNOW THAT? ...THIS STUFF THAT ...THEM INTO ...THEY MAKE A ...TO BE A ...HAVE TO GIV... ...NEW ...OUT. MAYBE ...AT'S

CLACK
CLICK
CLICK

WHAT ARE YOU BUSY BEES UP TO?

JUST DOUBLE-CHECKING AN EXPENSE REPORT... I DIDN'T HAVE TIME TO FINISH IT AT THE OFFICE.

CLICK
CLACK
CLICK

BLECH!

PLEASE TELL ME YOU'RE DOING SOMETHING LESS SPREADSHEET-Y.

I'M LOOKING AT THE WEBSITE FOR A FILM FESTIVAL THAT SOMEONE FROM THE COMMUNITY CENTER IS ORGANIZING!

THEY'RE LOOKING FOR SHORT FILM SUBMISSIONS FROM CREATORS OF ALL AGES.

DOES THIS MEAN YOU'RE MOVING ON FROM YOUR GUITAR-LESSONS PHASE?

OH, IT BETTER NOT.

THIS ISN'T GOING TO TURN INTO A REPEAT OF THE KARATE-LESSONS INCIDENT.

OLIVE TOOK KARATE LESSONS?

FOR EXACTLY A WEEK AND A HALF.

SHE BEGGED ME TO SIGN HER UP BECAUSE TRENT AND SAWYER TAKE KARATE.

I BOUGHT HER THE GI, AND FOUND HER A CLASS, AND REARRANGED MY SCHEDULE TO TAKE HER TO THE DOJO...

AND THEN AFTER **THREE** CLASSES SHE DECIDED SHE "JUST WASN'T FEELING IT."

WHEN I BOUGHT YOU THE GUITAR, YOU PROMISED ME YOU'D STICK WITH IT UNTIL AT LEAST THE END OF THE SCHOOL YEAR.

I KNOW, MOM.

I'M NOT QUITTING GUITAR.

THE FESTIVAL IS LOOKING FOR **SHORT** FILMS. I CAN MAKE SOMETHING IN MY SPARE TIME.

DOES THIS MEAN YOU NEED A VIDEO CAMERA?

IT MIGHT NOT BE STATE-OF-THE-ART, BUT OLIVE COULD BORROW A CAMERA FROM THE LIBRARY.

THAT SOUNDS PERFECT.

THANKS, MOL.

ARE YOU OKAY, WILLOW?

I'M FINE...

IT'S JUST...MY PARENTS SIGNED ME UP FOR BERRY SCOUTS.

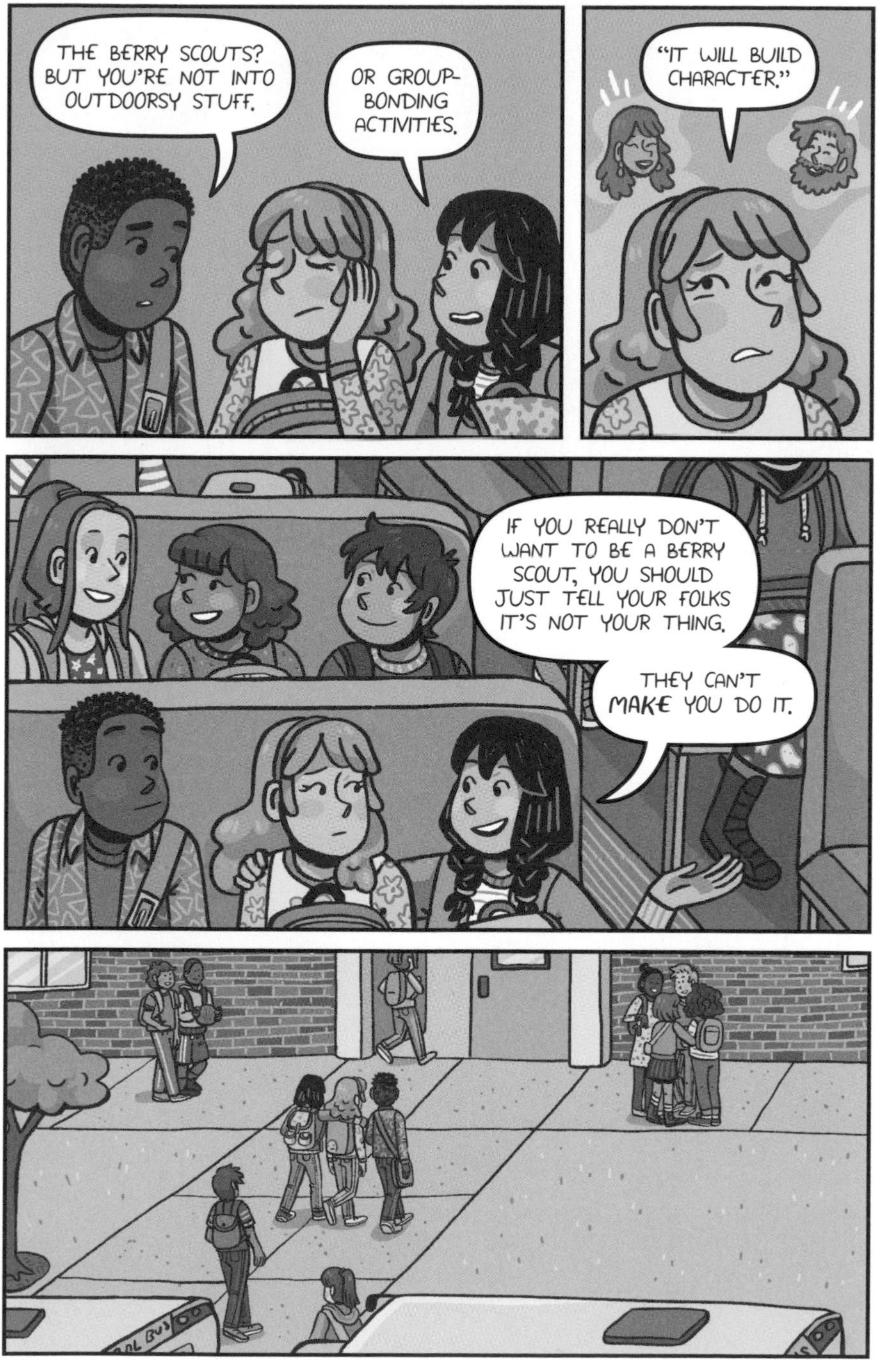
THE BERRY SCOUTS? BUT YOU'RE NOT INTO OUTDOORSY STUFF.
OR GROUP-BONDING ACTIVITIES.
"IT WILL BUILD CHARACTER."
IF YOU REALLY DON'T WANT TO BE A BERRY SCOUT, YOU SHOULD JUST TELL YOUR FOLKS IT'S NOT YOUR THING.
THEY CAN'T MAKE YOU DO IT.

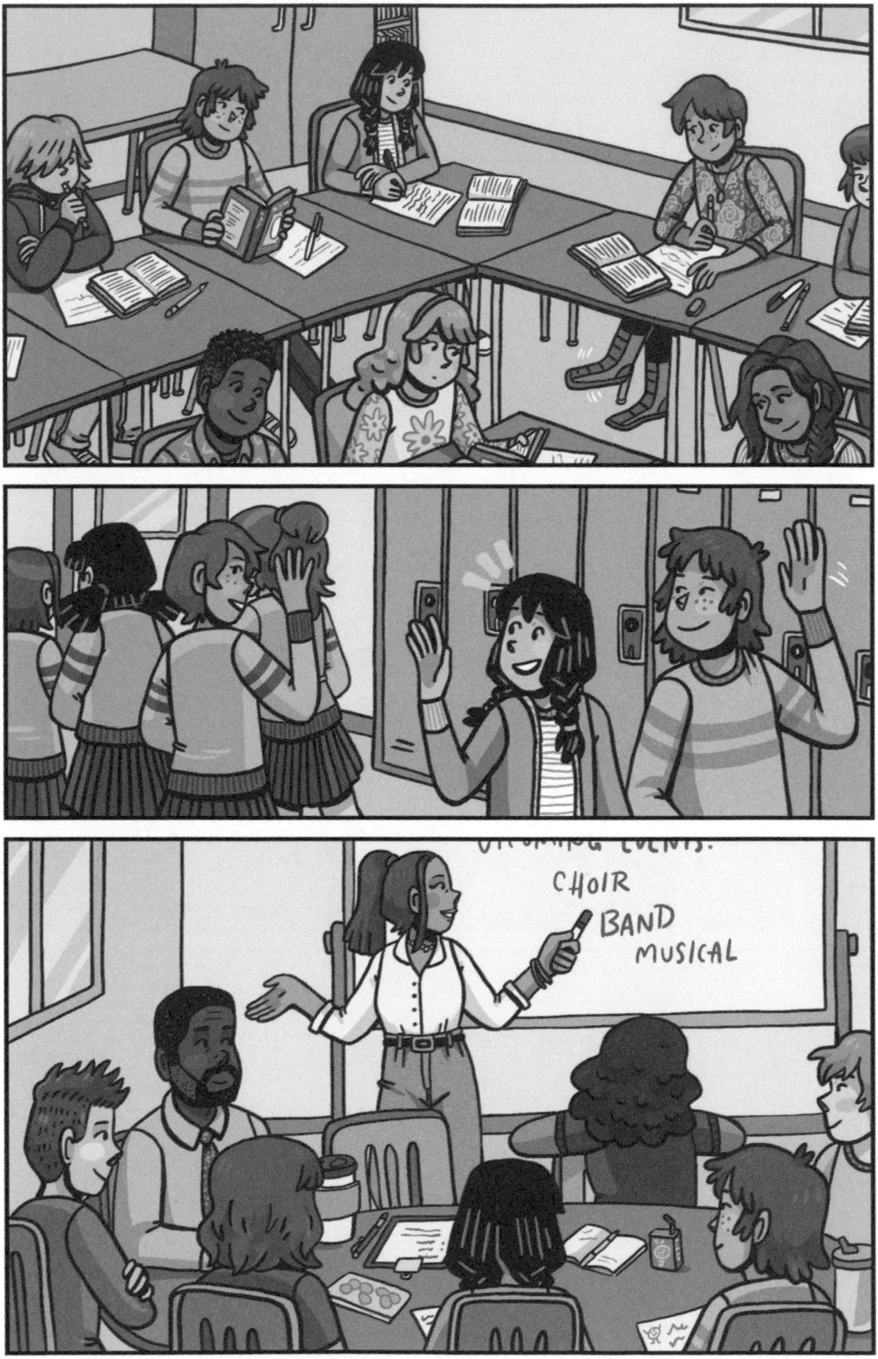
CHOIR
BAND
MUSICAL

WELL, THAT ABOUT COVERS EVERYTHING. DOES ANYONE HAVE ANYTHING ELSE THEY'D LIKE TO ADD?

UPCOMING EVEN

CHOIR

B

YES, OLIVE?

I WAS WONDERING IF WE COULD REVIEW THE SCHOOL DRESS CODE?

I KNOW SOME STUDENTS THINK IT'S...A BIT UNFAIR.

TRY "TYRANNICAL."

THE CURRENT DRESS CODE HAS BEEN ON THE BOOKS SINCE BEFORE I WAS PRINCIPAL. I'D BE OPEN TO UPDATING IT.

TRENT, YOU AND OLIVE WORK WELL TOGETHER...

WHY DON'T YOU TWO GATHER SOME INFO ON HOW STUDENTS FEEL ABOUT THE DRESS CODE AND PRESENT IT TO THE GROUP?

TEAM OLIVE AND TRENT...

CLAP!

...LET'S GO!

Today is a Good Day...

I THINK THE CHEER SQUAD WOULD BE A GOOD PLACE TO START—

TRENT!

LIV!

WHAT ARE YOU GUYS TALKING ABOUT?

THE DRESS CODE. MS. LIN WANTS US TO ASK AROUND AND SEE HOW KIDS FEEL ABOUT IT.

I'M GOING TO TALK TO THE CHEERLEADERS TOMORROW.

AND I WANT TO POLL THE GUYS IN OUR CLASS.

I COULD INQUIRE AMONGST MY ADVENTURERS' GUILD.

IF YOU MEAN "ASK YOUR RPG CLUB," THAT WOULD BE AWESOME, SAWYER.

THANKS.

15

MOM, I'M HOME!

HELLO, SWEETHEART.

MONSTER MOVIE SCRIPT

SCENE 1:

WILLOW CALLED.

I'M WORKING ON SOMETHING. I'LL SEE HER TOMORROW.

THREE TIMES.

THREE TIMES?

UH-HUH, SHE'S UPSET ABOUT FRUIT RANGERS OR SOMETHING.

FRUIT RANGERS?

OH! BERRY SCOUTS, I'D BETTER CALL HER BACK.

RIIING! RIIING!

HELLO?

HEY, WIL—

OLIVE!

YOU HAVE TO COME OVER FOR DINNER!

WHY? WHAT'S WRONG?

EVERYTHING!

I KEEP TRYING TO TELL MY PARENTS THAT I DON'T WANT TO BE A BERRY SCOUT, BUT I—

I JUST CAN'T! I CAN'T GET A WORD IN.

YOU'RE SO MUCH BETTER AT THIS KIND OF THING...

I NEED YOU TO HELP ME!

I DON'T KNOW...

PLEASE Please Please PLEASE PLEASE PLEASE Please PLEASE Please PLEASE please PLEASE

OKAY, OKAY.

GREAT. DINNER IS IN TEN MINUTES.

CLICK.

HELLO, OLIVE.

WILLOW IS UP IN HER ROOM.

OOOOH, GIRL, YOU ARE A TIGER!

AND TONIGHT, NO ONE'S BURNING BRIGHTER!

WILLOW? WHAT ARE YOU DOING?

GIRL, YOU ARE A-

I WAS JUST TRYING TO GET PUMPED UP BEFORE WE CONFRONT MY PARENTS.

I THINK YOU'RE GETTING MORE WORKED UP ABOUT THIS THAN YOU HAVE TO.

YOU SAY THAT NOW, BUT YOU'LL SEE. YOU'LL SEE...

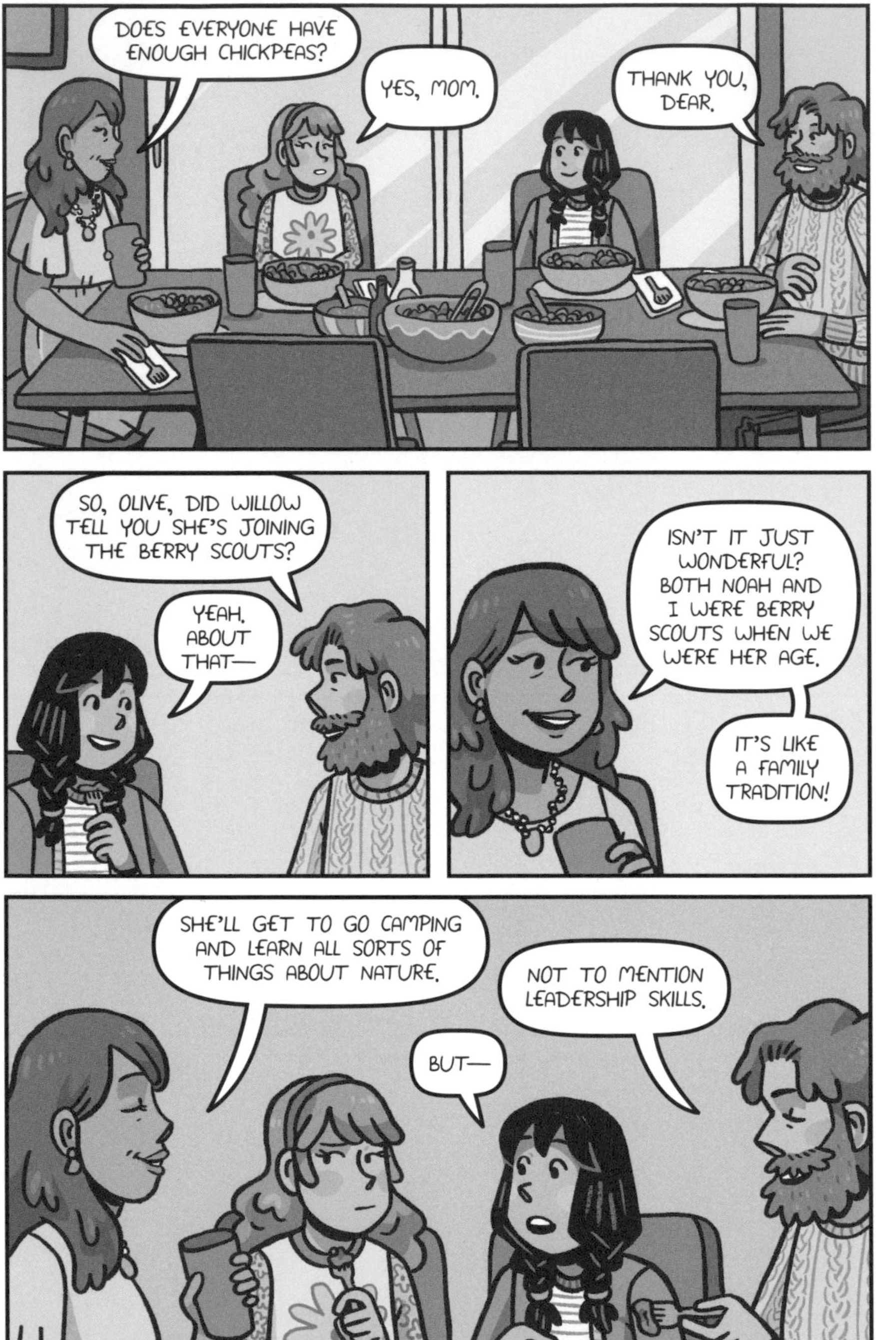

DOES EVERYONE HAVE ENOUGH CHICKPEAS?
YES, MOM.
THANK YOU, DEAR.
SO, OLIVE, DID WILLOW TELL YOU SHE'S JOINING THE BERRY SCOUTS?
YEAH. ABOUT THAT—
ISN'T IT JUST WONDERFUL? BOTH NOAH AND I WERE BERRY SCOUTS WHEN WE WERE HER AGE.
IT'S LIKE A FAMILY TRADITION!
SHE'LL GET TO GO CAMPING AND LEARN ALL SORTS OF THINGS ABOUT NATURE.
BUT—
NOT TO MENTION LEADERSHIP SKILLS.

YOU KNOW, IF YOU STICK WITH THE BERRY SCOUTS LONG ENOUGH, YOU CAN EVEN PUT IT ON YOUR COLLEGE APPLICATION.

HAVE YOU EVER THOUGHT OF JOINING THE BERRY SCOUTS, OLIVE?

WELL, I—

THAT'S A WONDERFUL IDEA! YOU HAD A GREAT TIME AT SUMMER CAMP TOGETHER.

I—UMM...

I GUESS... IT MIGHT BE FUN?

YAY!

YOU TWO ARE GOING TO LOVE BEING SCOUTS.

I'LL EMAIL YOUR MOM THE SIGN-UP FORM!

BYE, OLIVE.

OKAY, THANKS, MR. VOSS.

HOW'D IT GO, JELLY BEAN?

I MIGHT HAVE ACCIDENTALLY AGREED TO JOIN THE BERRY SCOUTS WITH WILLOW.

WHAT?!

I CAN PAY FOR THE MEMBERSHIP DUES WITH MY OWN MONEY...

AND WILLOW'S PARENTS WILL DRIVE ME. YOU DON'T HAVE TO WORRY ABOUT ANYTHING.

I'M NOT WORRIED ABOUT THE MONEY, OLIVE.

YOU JUST HAVE SO MANY THINGS ON YOUR PLATE ALREADY. SCHOOL, STUDENT COUNCIL, GUITAR LESSONS...

IF YOU JOIN BERRY SCOUTS TOO, YOU'RE NOT GOING TO HAVE MUCH FREE TIME—

ESPECIALLY IF YOU'RE SERIOUS ABOUT MAKING A SHORT FILM ON TOP OF ALL THAT.

IT'S OKAY, MOM. I LIKE BEING BUSY!

HOW DID TALKING TO YOUR PARENTS GO, WILLOW?

WELL...

YOU'RE LOOKING AT NOT ONE BUT **TWO** FUTURE BERRY SCOUTS.

NO WAY!

WILLOW'S PARENTS ARE VERY... **CONVINCING**.

MAYBE THEY COULD PERSUADE YOU TO SIGN UP TOO, HUGH.

IT BUILDS CHARACTER, REMEMBER?

NUH-UH. NOT INTERESTED. I'VE BUILT UP ALL THE CHARACTER I NEED.

WHAT'S TRENT UP TO?

HUH?

SCENE 2:

HE'S QUIZZING ALL THE GUYS ON SOMETHING...

OH, HE'S PROBABLY ASKING THEM ABOUT THE DRESS CODE.

WHY?

THE STUDENT COUNCIL IS GOING TO WORK WITH MS. LIN TO UPDATE IT. ACTUALLY, AVA, I WANTED TO TALK—

ALL RIGHT, CLASS, PLEASE TAKE OUT YOUR READING JOURNALS.

TO BE CONTINUED?

OKAY.

HAVE ANY OF YOU EVER GOTTEN A WARNING OR DETENTION OVER A DRESS-CODE VIOLATION?

I'VE NEVER HAD AN ISSUE.

NEITHER HAVE I.

I'VE NEVER GOTTEN A DETENTION, BUT I DID GET A "STERN WARNING" ABOUT ONE OF MY TOPS. I'VE KEPT A SPARE CARDIGAN IN MY LOCKER EVER SINCE.

YOU NEVER TOLD ME THAT! WHICH TOP?

CHARTREUSE WITH DAISIES. THE VINTAGE ONE.

GASP!

RIDICULOUS! I *LOVE* THAT SHIRT!

I GOT A DETENTION LAST WEEK FOR WEARING LEGGINGS AS PANTS...

EVEN THOUGH THE SWEATER I WAS WEARING WENT HALFWAY DOWN MY THIGHS.

BUT WAS IT MORE THAN THREE INCHES ABOVE YOUR KNEES?

FIRST WEEK OF SCHOOL: IT WAS HOT, I WORE SHORTS.

GOT STOPPED, AND A TEACHER ACTUALLY USED A RULER TO CHECK HOW MANY INCHES OF MY LEG WERE SHOWING.

DO YOU SEE HOW LONG MY LEGS ARE?

IF I WANTED TO BUY SHORTS THAT WENT TO MY KNEES, I'D NEED TO SHOP IN THE CAPRIS SECTION!

HOW ABOUT YOU, NAT?

DO YOU HAVE ANY VIOLATIONS ON YOUR RECORD?

WHERE SHOULD I START?

RIPPED JEANS, BARE SHOULDERS, VISIBLE BRA STRAPS, CROPPED TOPS, SHORT SHORTS, OPEN-TOED SHOES, EXPOSED COLLARBONES...

DID YOU GET DETENTIONS FOR ALL OF THOSE?

SOME OF THEM. I'D RATHER GET A FEW DETENTIONS THAN RETIRE MY FAVORITE SWEATER AND DESIGNER DISTRESSED JEANS.

BESIDES, THE DRESS CODE IS ENFORCED PRETTY INCONSISTENTLY. I GET AWAY WITH WEARING WHATEVER I WANT 50% OF THE TIME.

DON'T YOUR PARENTS GET MAD THAT YOU KEEP GETTING IN TROUBLE?

NOT REALLY.

WHO DO YOU THINK PAYS FOR MY CLOTHES?

HAVE YOU EVER HAD A DRESS-CODE ISSUE, LIV?

NO...

YOU'LL HAVE TO LOOK OUT IF THEY DECIDE TO BAN T-SHIRTS AND JEANS.

HA HA HA

DID YOU TALK TO THE CHEERLEADERS ABOUT DRESS-CODE STUFF TODAY?

YEAH, BETH AND CHANDA, TOO.

DID YOU TALK TO THE GUYS?

YEAH.

THEY DIDN'T HAVE A TON TO SAY, BUT I TOOK NOTES.

WHAT DID—

AHEM!

DID WE COME HERE TO TALK...

...OR DID WE COME HERE TO SKATE?

CLICK!

30

WANT TO COME OVER TOMORROW AND EXCHANGE NOTES?

TOMORROW IS A NO-GO—

I HAVE MY FIRST-EVER BERRY SCOUT MEETING.

SUNDAY? DOES SUNDAY WORK FOR YOU, SAWYER?

I DON'T HAVE ANY NOTES TO EXCHANGE. THE RPG CLUB HASN'T HAD ANY BATTLES WITH THE DRESS CODE—

ONLY ORCS AND GOBLINS.

MAYBE I'LL ASK NAT IF SHE WANTS TO HIT THE MALL ON SUNDAY...

SMOOCH SMOOCH

OOOOOOOH! HOW ROMANTIC!

HEY!

MOM, HOW PARTIAL ARE YOU TO THOSE OLD GREEN TOWELS IN THE LINEN CLOSET?

THEY'RE NOT MY FAVORITE. WHY?

I WAS WONDERING IF I COULD **UPCYCLE** THEM FOR MY MOVIE.

PLEASE? IN THE NAME OF ART?

EXACTLY HOW MANY TOWELS NEED TO BECOME ART?

HMM...DOESN'T SEEM LIKE A LOT OF HOMEWORK IS GETTING DONE TODAY.

STRANGE, CONSIDERING SOMEONE HAS A BERRY SCOUT MEETING THIS AFTERNOON AND ASKED TO GO TO A FRIEND'S HOUSE TOMORROW.

MESSAGE RECEIVED. HOMEWORK SEQUENCE INITIATED.

HI THERE! ARE THOSE OUR NEW BERRY SCOUTS I SEE?

I'M TODD, THIS BUSH'S ELDERBERRY—OR THIS TROOP'S SCOUT LEADER, FOR THOSE NOT YET HIP TO BERRY SCOUT LINGO.

HELLO, I'M OLIVE, AND THIS IS WILLOW.

AND I'M MISTY, AND THIS IS NOAH. I BELIEVE WE SPOKE ON THE PHONE?

NICE TO MEET YOU IN PERSON.

I HAVE SOME READING MATERIAL FOR YOU PARENTS TO TAKE HOME...

...AND WE'LL SEE YOU AT FOUR FOR PICKUP WHEN THE MEETING ENDS.

YOU MEAN WE CAN'T STAY?

WE'RE CURRENTLY ALL GOOD ON THE PARENT VOLUNTEER FRONT, BUT IF YOU WANTED TO STICK AROUND FOR THE GIRLS' FIRST MEETING... WELL, IT'S A PUBLIC PARK.

GATHER ROUND, EVERYBERRY!

AS SOME OF YOU MORE OBSERVANT SCOUTS MAY HAVE NOTICED, WE HAVE TWO NEW BLUEBERRIES JOINING OUR BUSH THIS AFTERNOON!

WILLOW, OLIVE, WHY DON'T YOU BOTH COME UP AND TELL US ABOUT YOURSELVES?

HEY! I'M OLIVE. I'M A SIXTH GRADER. I'M ON MY SCHOOL'S STUDENT COUNCIL.

I LIKE SKATEBOARDING, ART, AND SOFTBALL— AND I'M LEARNING GUITAR.

MY NAME IS WILLOW. I'M ALSO IN SIXTH GRADE, AND I...

UHH...

LIKE VIDEO GAMES AND WATCHING SCARY MOVIES.

WE'RE VERY HAPPY TO HAVE YOU BOTH WITH US. RIGHT, EVERYBERRY?

NOW, LET'S GET DOWN TO BUSINESS. THE WILDERNESS CAN BE A DANGEROUS PLACE, AND IT'S IMPORTANT TO BE EDUCATED AND PREPARED.

EVEN THE MOST CAUTIOUS AND DILIGENT SCOUTS CAN FIND THEMSELVES INJURED AND IN SERIOUS NEED OF SOME...?

CAN ANYONE GUESS?

MAYBE ONE OF OUR NEW BERRIES.

OLIVE? YOU'VE BEEN TAKING A LOT OF NOTES.

UHHH...

FIRST AID

FIRST AID!

VERY GOOD, OLIVE... OR SHOULD I SAY, **WILLOW.**

TODAY WE'LL BE LEARNING HOW TO DEAL WITH ONE OF THE MOST COMMON INJURIES THAT HAPPEN DURING HIKES: SPRAINED ANKLES.

LONG STORY SHORT: YOU'RE GOING TO WANT TO REST, PUT SOME ICE ON IT, MAYBE WRAP IT IN A BANDAGE DEPENDING ON HOW MUCH IT HURTS, AND PROP THAT BABY UP ON A PILLOW.

BUT IF YOU'RE IN THE MIDDLE OF A HIKE, YOU PROBABLY DON'T HAVE A TON OF ICE PACKS AND PILLOWS HANDY.

WHICH IS WHY TODAY WE'LL BE PRACTICING—

THE TWO-PERSON CARRY!

THAT'S RIGHT! WE'RE GONNA DO A TWO-PERSON-CARRY RACE SO WE CAN ALL LEARN HOW TO GET AN INJURED FRIEND TO SAFETY.

GROUPS OF THREE!

LET'S GO!

HEY, WE COULD PUT EACH OF YOU IN A GROUP WITH TWO OF US SINCE WE ALREADY KNOW THE DRILL.

CAN'T WE BE ON A TEAM TOGETHER?

I GUESS SO? I CAN BE YOUR THIRD PERSON.

I'M TARA, BY THE WAY.

DON'T DROP ME, DON'T DROP ME, DON'T DROP ME!

WE'RE NOT GOING TO DROP YOU.

AND IF WE DID DROP YOU, AT LEAST THERE ARE PLENTY OF PEOPLE WHO COULD CARRY YOU TO THE CAR.

HEH.

GOOD HUSTLE TODAY, SCOUTS.

YOU'LL HAVE AN OPPORTUNITY TO EARN YOUR FIRST-AID MERIT BADGE NEXT WEEKEND, SO STUDY THOSE GUIDEBOOKS.

EACH PAIR OF SCOUTS WILL HAVE TO PERFORM ONE FIRST-AID TECHNIQUE... BUT I'M NOT TELLING YOU WHICH ONE YOU'LL GET BEFOREHAND.

BLUEBERRIES MIGHT WANT TO TEAM UP WITH MORE EXPERIENCED SCOUTS FOR THE TEST!

DAD, CAN WE GET TACOS FOR DINNER?

I'M TWO-PERSON HUNGRY.

HEY, I'M AJ—
DID EITHER OF YOU NEED A BUDDY FOR THE TEST?

NO THANKS, WE'RE GOOD.

OKAAAY.

DID YOU TWO HAVE FUN? IT SEEMED EXCITING.

WHAT I HEARD SOUNDED PRETTY INFORMATIVE. THAT TODD GUY KNOWS HIS STUFF.

IT'S COOL THAT YOU CAN EARN A MERIT BADGE SO SOON!

YOU'LL HAVE TO WORK HARD, BUT YOU CAN DO IT.

HOW'D IT GO?

IT WAS FINE.

JUST FINE?

YEAH.

I HAD A GREAT IDEA FOR MY MOVIE, THOUGH!

I HAVE TO GO JOT IT DOWN.

REMEMBER OUR RULE: HOMEWORK FIRST!

HELLO, MR. PHAN.

HELLO, OLIVE.

TRENT IS INSI—

LIV! C'MON! I WANT TO GIVE YOU THE GRAND TOUR!

MY ROOM!

CAM'S ROOM!

THE KITCHEN!

ARE YOU TWO HUNGRY?

THE LIVING ROOM!

SO, WHAT DID YOU FIND OUT?

WELL—

WHATCHYA DOIN'? CAN I HELP?

SURE, CAM. C'MERE.

OLIVE AND I ARE TALKING ABOUT WHAT OUR FRIENDS ARE ALLOWED TO WEAR TO SCHOOL.

OKAY.

SO, ONLY TWO OF THE GUYS I SPOKE TO HAD ANY DRESS-CODE VIOLATIONS.

IVAN GOT STOPPED FOR WEARING A SHIRT WITH A POOP EMOJI ON IT.

THE TEACHER ASKED HIM TO PUT ON A SWEATSHIRT.

AND MR. MOSS GAVE ETHAN A WARNING FOR WEARING FLIP-FLOPS—

AFTER ETHAN TRIPPED AND ALMOST FELL DOWN THE STAIRS.

44

WOW— ALMOST EVERY GIRL I TALKED TO HAS GOTTEN AT LEAST A WARNING.

FOR WHAT?

ALL KINDS OF STUFF. SHORTS, LEGGINGS, TANK TOPS, SANDALS, RIPPED JEANS—

YOU NAME IT.

ONE TIME, AT PRESCHOOL, WE HAD A PAJAMA DAY AND EVERYONE GOT TO WEAR THEIR PJ'S *ALL* DAY LONG.

EVEN THE TEACHERS.

THANK YOU FOR YOUR INPUT.

YOU'RE VERY WELCOME.

BUH-BYE.

CHERISH THIS TIME WHILE IT LASTS, TRENT.

SOON ALL CAM WILL WANT TO DO IS BORROW YOUR STUFF AND MAKE SNARKY REMARKS.

SIMON ISN'T SO BAD.

HE'S A COOL LITTLE DUDE.

HMPH.

MAYBE YOU SHOULD TAKE THE LEAD ON THIS ONE?

IT SEEMS LIKE WAY MORE GIRLS HAVE BEEN AFFECTED BY THE DRESS CODE.

46

NOT THAT IT ISN'T SUPER INSULTING TO US GUYS WHEN TEACHERS ACT LIKE WE'LL SUDDENLY FORGET HOW TO READ IF WE SEE A GIRL'S **SHOULDER**...

BUT YOU KNOW— IF GIRLS ARE THE ONES GETTING IN TROUBLE, YOU PROBABLY HAVE MORE EXPERIENCE AND OPINIONS.

BUT *I* HAVEN'T BEEN PERSONALLY AFFECTED BY THE DRESS CODE EITHER.

SHOULD WE... ASK THE CHEER SQUAD TO TALK TO MS. LIN?

WE COULD DO A FASHION SHOW!

WE COULD HAVE PEOPLE WEAR THE OUTFITS THEY GOT IN TROUBLE FOR AND SHOW MS. LIN HOW SILLY SOME OF THE RULES ARE!

YES! THAT'S PERFECT!

WE'RE HOME!

WE'RE IN THE KITCHEN STARTING DINNER!

AUNT MOLLY AND GOOBER ARE COOKING?

OH NO.

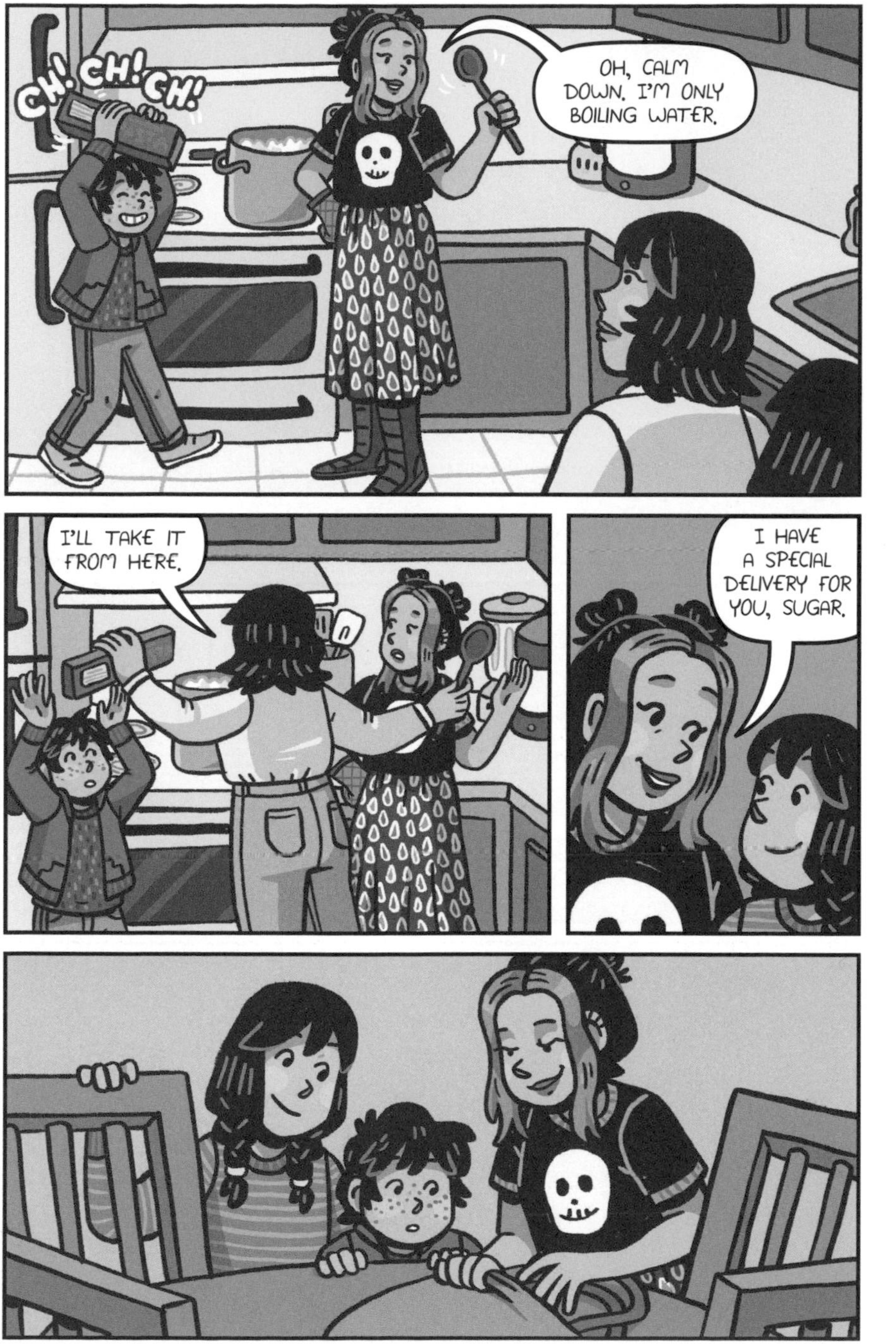
CH! CH! CH!
OH, CALM DOWN. I'M ONLY BOILING WATER.
I'LL TAKE IT FROM HERE.
I HAVE A SPECIAL DELIVERY FOR YOU, SUGAR.

IT'S NOT PRETTY, BUT IT'S IN WORKING ORDER.

LIBRARY

THANK YOU!

THANK YOU!

THANK YOU!

I CHECKED THIS STUFF OUT WITH YOUR LIBRARY CARD, SO YOU'RE RESPONSIBLE FOR IT.

THIS IS GREAT! I CAN'T WAIT TO START FILMING!

SO, WHAT IS YOUR MAGNUM OPUS GOING TO BE ABOUT?

IT'S A MONSTER MOVIE!

I HAVEN'T HAD MUCH TIME TO WORK ON THE SCRIPT YET...

...BUT I WANT IT TO BE ABOUT A SCIENTIST AND A COOL HERO GIRL WHO HAVE TO TEAM UP TO STOP A MONSTER!

OLIVE BRANCHE'S
MONSTER MOVIE

AND I GET TO BE THE MONSTER!

HA HA HA

GRR!

HA HA

COULD YOU PLEASE BE THE KIND OF MONSTER WHO EATS ALL OF THEIR DINNER?

GOOD MORNING! WE SORT OF HAVE A FAVOR TO ASK YOU—

BUT HOPEFULLY A FUN FAVOR?

WE WANT TO PROVE THAT SOME OF THE DRESS-CODE RULES ARE UNFAIR, AND SINCE SOME OF YOU HAVE BEEN AFFECTED DIRECTLY...

...WE WERE WONDERING IF YOU'D HELP US PUT ON A FASHION SHOW!

WE HAVE TO RUN IT BY MS. LIN, BUT OUR IDEA IS THAT YOU COULD WEAR OUTFITS THAT YOU DON'T THINK YOU SHOULD HAVE GOTTEN IN TROUBLE FOR AND WALK THE RUNWAY AT A STUDENT COUNCIL MEETING.

WE **LOVE** FASHION SHOWS.

SOUNDS LIKE FUN.

I'M IN.

WHATEVER.

OLIVE, DO YOU WANT TO COME OVER AND PRACTICE FOR THE FIRST-AID MERIT BADGE TEST? YOU COULD COME TOO, HUGH.

SOUNDS GOOD! I HAD SOMETHING I WANTED TO TALK TO YOU TWO ABOUT ANYWAY.

OKAY, SO THIS IS EVERYTHING THE BERRY SCOUT HANDBOOK RECOMMENDS YOU KEEP IN YOUR BASIC FIRST-AID KIT.

THIS IS THE **BASIC** STUFF?

IF YOU WERE REALLY GOING OUT INTO THE WILDERNESS, YOU'D WANT TO BRING ALONG A LOT MORE, BUT THIS IS ALL THE STUFF WE'LL NEED FOR ANY OF THE SKILLS WE MIGHT BE TESTED ON.

THERE ARE ABOUT 15 TECHNIQUES WE NEED TO KNOW.

I CAN SHOW YOU THE ONES I'VE ALREADY BEEN STUDYING. HUGH, DO YOU MIND IF I PRACTICE ON YOU?

TO SPLINT AN INJURED FINGER, FIRST YOU TAKE A POPSICLE STICK...

...AND YOU...

...YOU PUT IT THERE...

OH, WAIT.

YOU'RE SUPPOSED TO TRIM IT DOWN...

...BUT I DON'T KNOW IF MY SCISSORS...

...I COULD JUST...

...MAYBE IF...

SO, WHAT DID YOU WANT TO TALK TO US ABOUT?

I WAS WONDERING IF YOU'D WANT TO STAR IN MY MONSTER MOVIE!

MONSTER MOVIE?!

I'M MAKING A SHORT FILM FOR THIS FESTIVAL AT THE COMMUNITY CENTER. I WAS THINKING YOU TWO COULD PLAY THE BRILLIANT SCIENTIST AND THE KICK-BUTT HERO GIRL.

I DON'T KNOW, OLIVE.

YOU KNOW I'M NOT VERY GOOD IN FRONT OF A CAMERA.

WOW.

I CAN'T MOVE MY FINGERS AT ALL.

IMMOBILIZING THE INJURED FINGER IS THE POINT OF A SPLINT.

AND IF YOU WANT TO IMMOBILIZE AN INJURED ARM, YOU CAN MAKE A SLING OUT OF A SHIRT.

YOU JUST HAVE TO PUT YOUR HEAD THROUGH...

...AND YOU PULL IT...

THEN YOU MOVE IT SORT OF LIKE THAT...

...AND THEN YOU...

I REALLY WANT YOU TO BE IN THE MOVIE, WILLOW.

IT'LL BE FUN TO MAKE SOMETHING TOGETHER.

PLUS, IT'S A **SHORT** FILM, SO YOU WOULDN'T HAVE TO LEARN TOO MANY LINES.

CAN WE READ THE SCRIPT?

I'M STILL WORKING ON IT.

ARE YOU GOING TO PLAY THE MONSTER?

NO, GOOBER IS—

AND I WANT TO DO SOME STOP-MOTION STUFF, TOO!

AHEM.

WE'RE SUPPOSED TO BE PRACTICING FIRST-AID TECHNIQUES.

ADHESIVE BANDAGES

SORRY, WILLOW.

I'M JUST REALLY EXCITED ABOUT THIS.

YOU ROCK

IT'S OKAY. I KNOW YOU ONLY JOINED THE BERRY SCOUTS BECAUSE MY PARENTS USED THEIR MIND-CONTROL POWERS...

WHAT IF I DO ALL THE RESEARCH AND TAKE NOTES, AND IN EXCHANGE YOU DO ALL THE TALKING DURING THE TEST?

IF THAT WORKS FOR YOU, IT WORKS FOR ME!

DOES THIS MEAN WE CAN KEEP TALKING ABOUT THE MONSTER MOVIE?

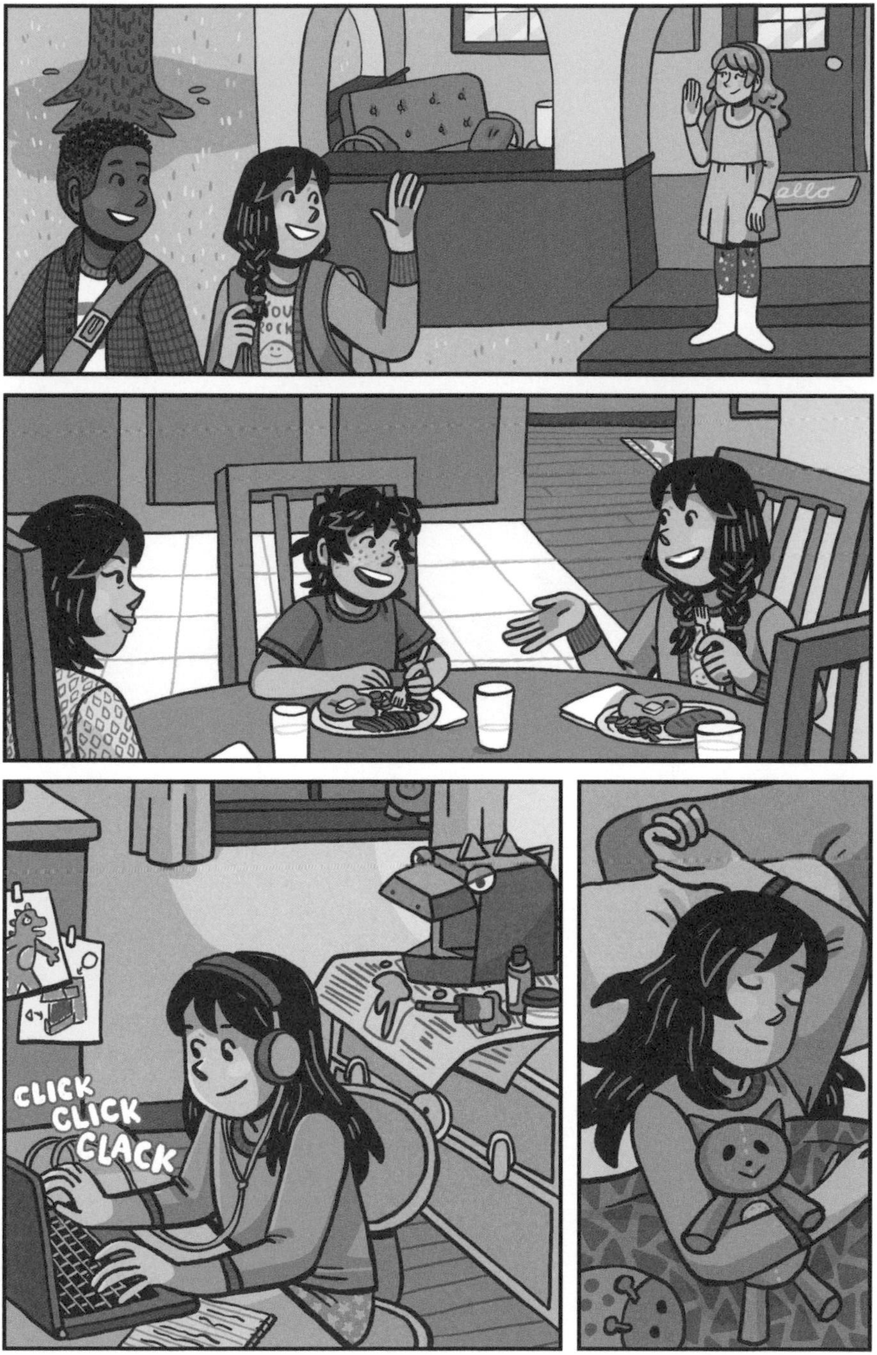
CLICK
CLICK
CLACK

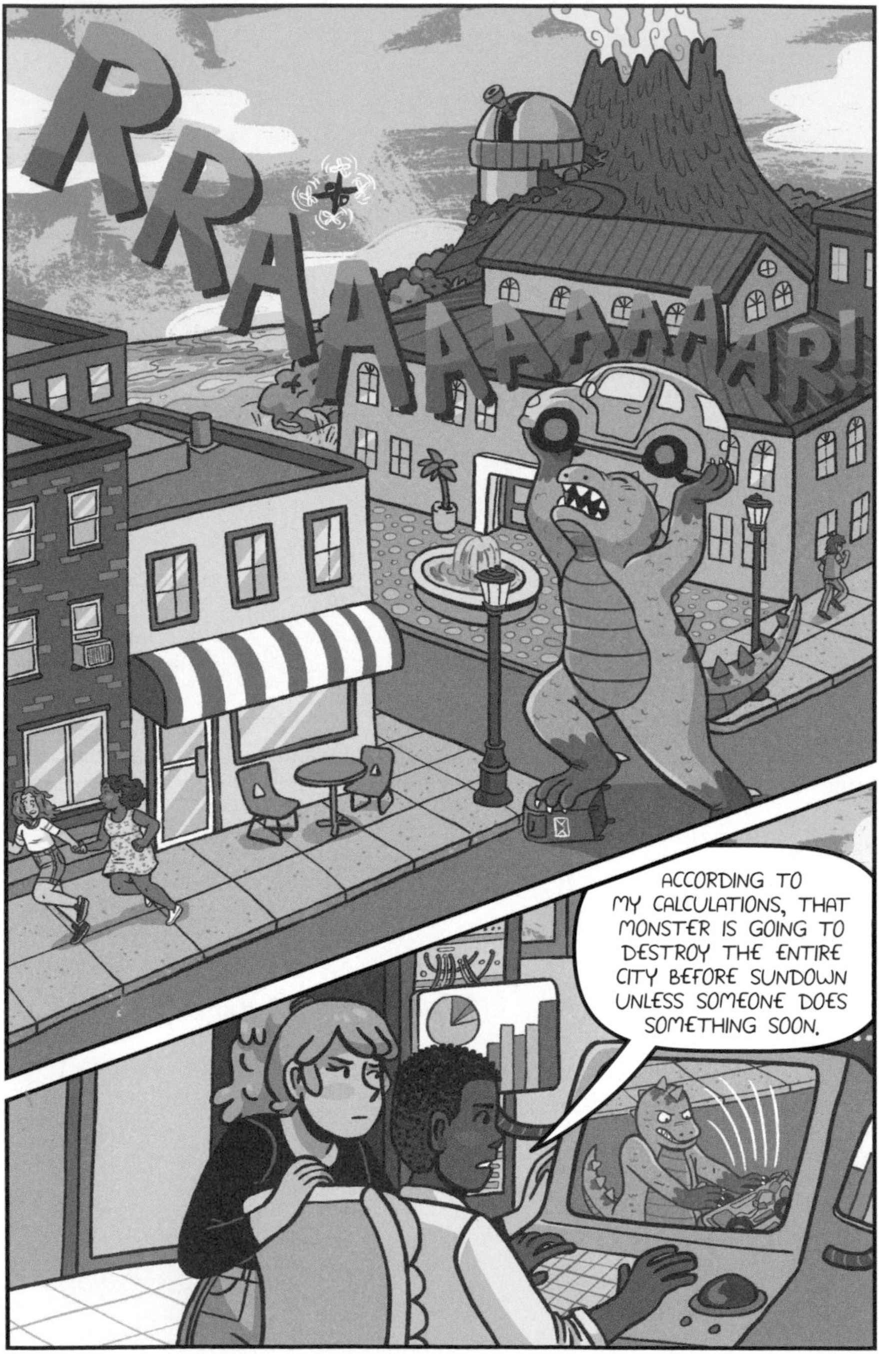
RRAAAAAAAAR!
ACCORDING TO MY CALCULATIONS, THAT MONSTER IS GOING TO DESTROY THE ENTIRE CITY BEFORE SUNDOWN UNLESS SOMEONE DOES SOMETHING SOON.

IT'S MY DUTY TO PROTECT THIS ISLAND AND EVERYONE ON IT.

I HAVE TO GET OUT THERE.

YOU KNOW I'VE GOT YOUR BACK.

CRASH!

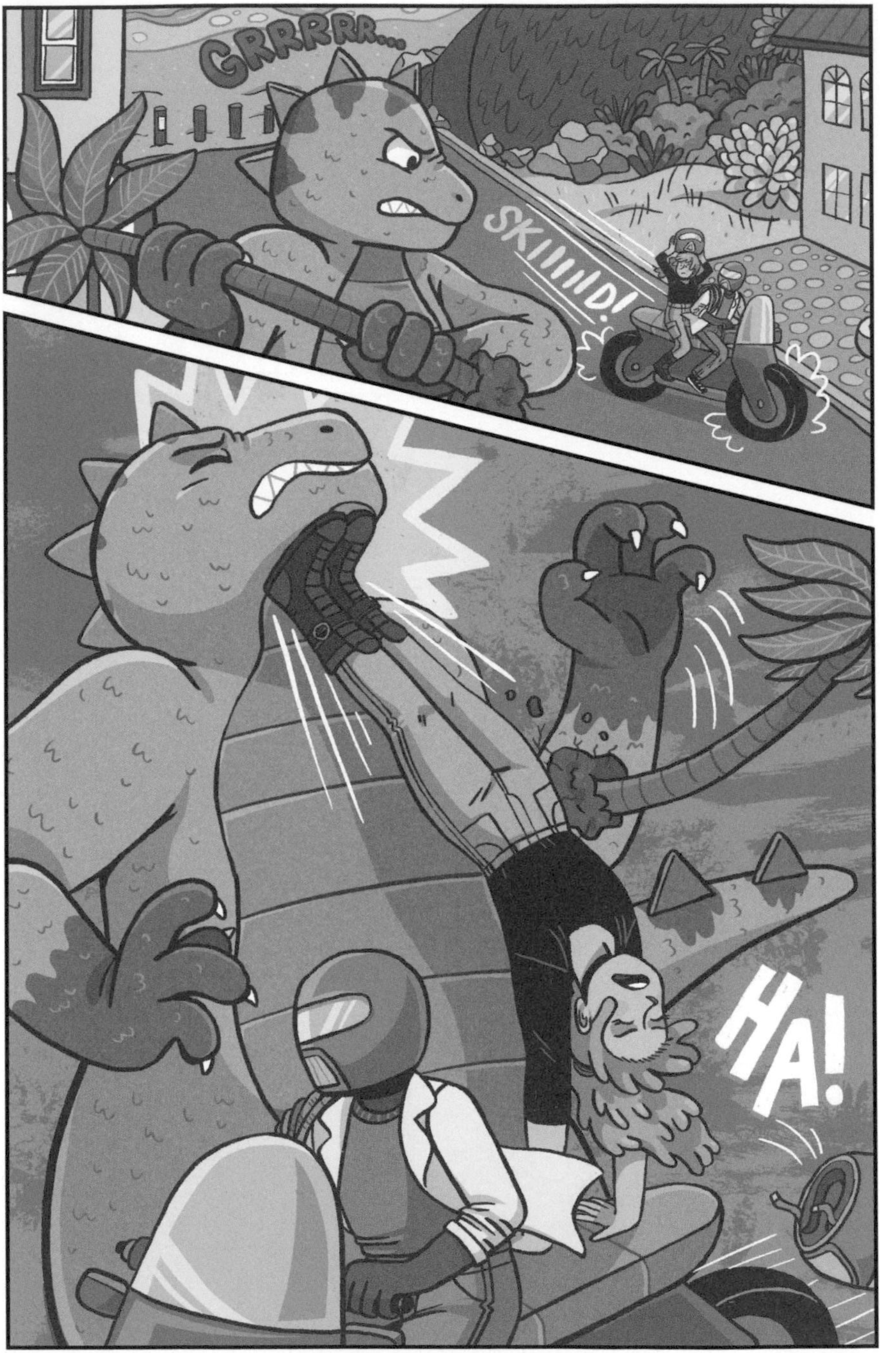
GRRRRR...
SKIIIIID!
HA!

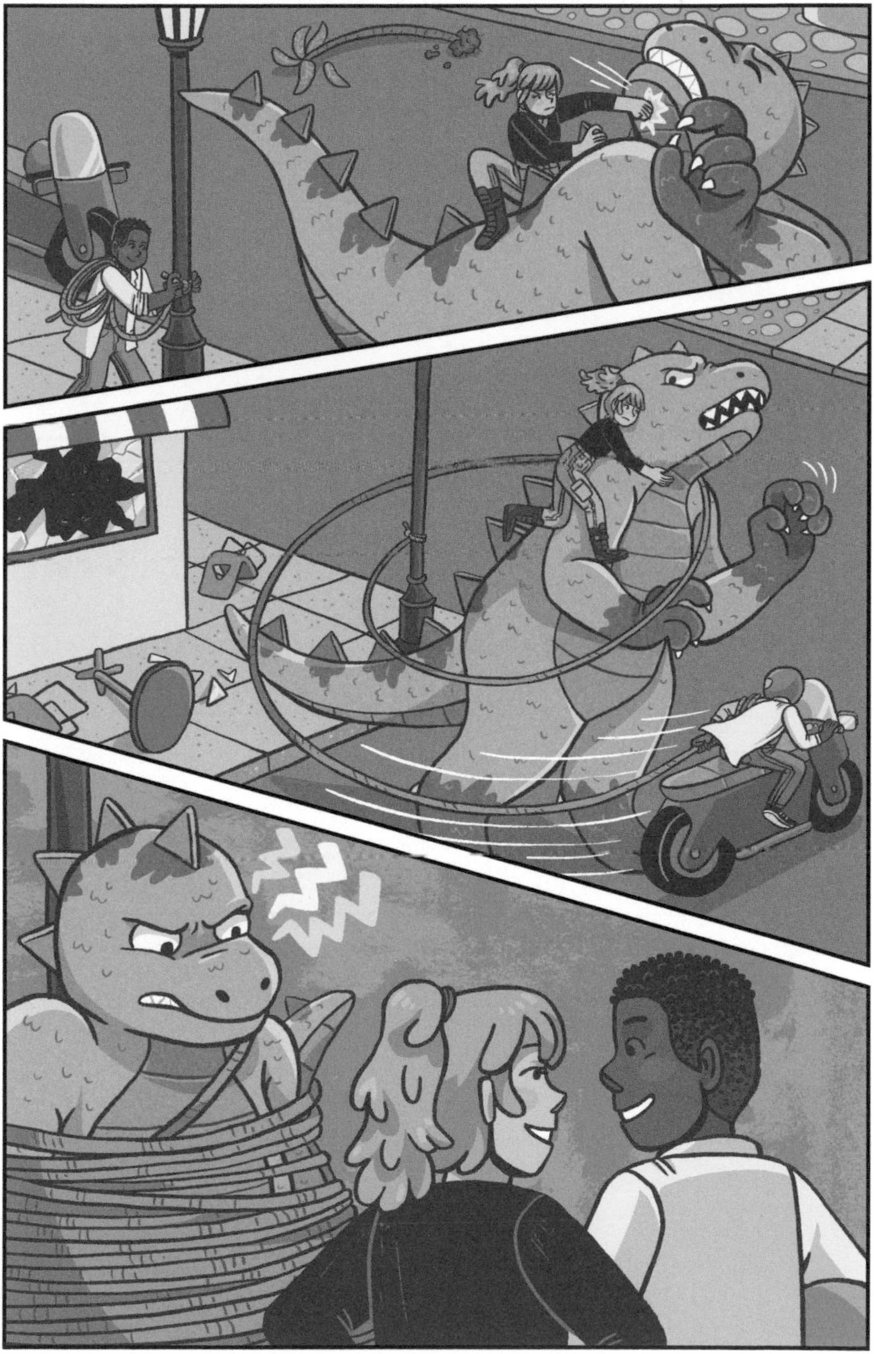

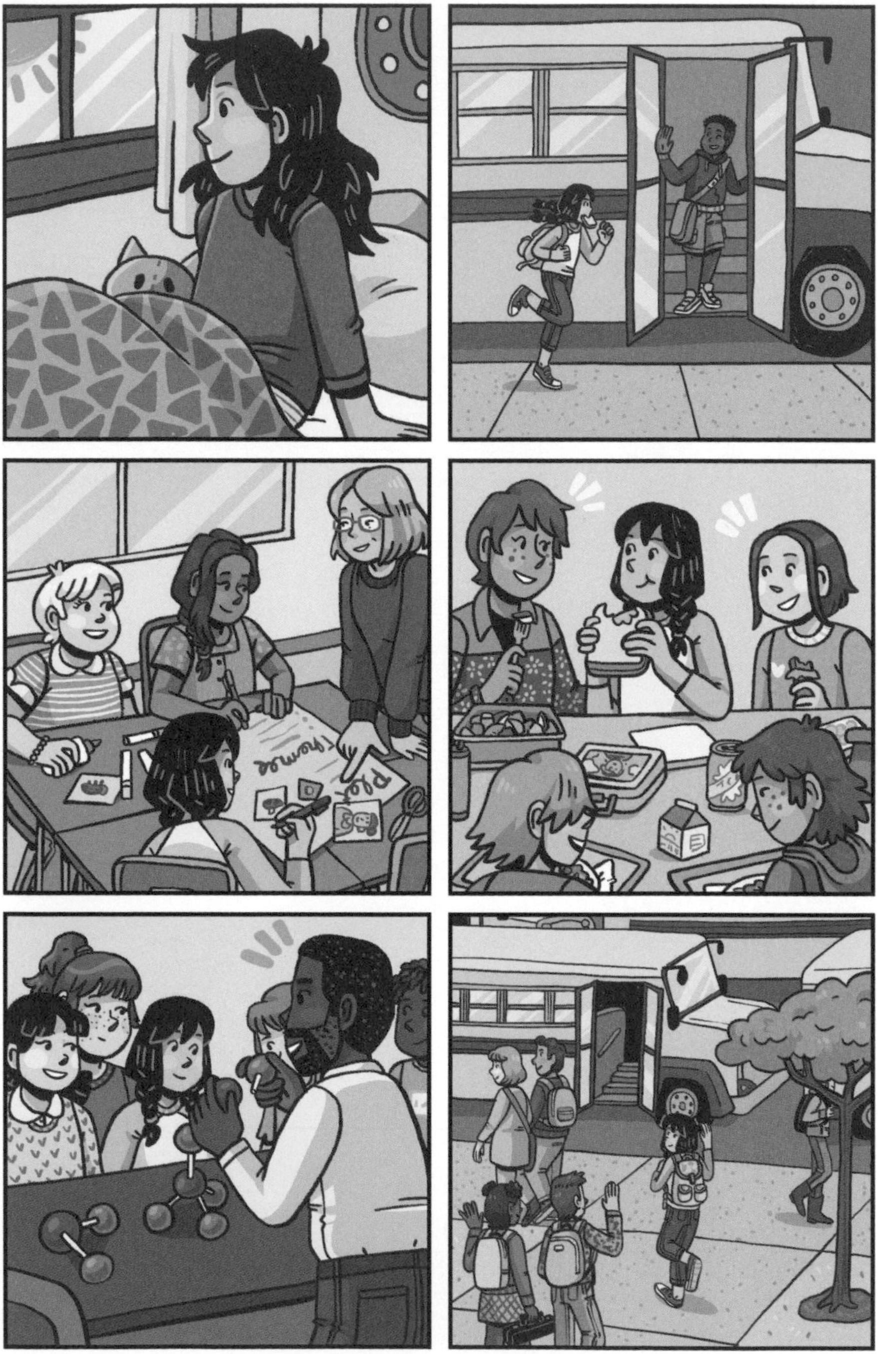

WHAT ARE YOU WORKING ON?

GETTING A HEAD START ON MY SCIENCE HOMEWORK.

I'VE GOT A LOT GOING ON, SO IT'S IMPORTANT THAT I STAY ORGANIZED AND MANAGE MY TIME WISELY.

IS THAT WHAT YOU WERE DOING WHEN YOU ALMOST MISSED THE BUS THIS MORNING?

THERE'S NO SUCH THING AS **TIME** IN THE **MORNING**.

HEY, MOM, I'M HOME!

WAIT, COULD YOU COME HERE A SECOND?

HOW MANY HOURS HAVE YOU PRACTICED YOUR GUITAR THIS WEEK?

UMM...

YOU'RE SUPPOSED TO PRACTICE FOR THREE HOURS A WEEK...AND YOUR NEXT LESSON IS TOMORROW.

NO PROBLEM.

I CAN PRACTICE FOR THREE HOURS TONIGHT!

I THINK IT WOULD BE EASIER TO PRACTICE HALF AN HOUR EVERY DAY BETWEEN LESSONS INSTEAD OF PUTTING IT OFF UNTIL THE LAST MINUTE. OR EVEN ONE HOUR A DAY FOR THREE DAYS.

I CAN TRY THAT NEXT WEEK!

DO YOU WANT ME TO GET YOU A CALENDAR? OR A POCKET PLANNER?

WE CAN TALK ABOUT THAT LATER—RIGHT NOW IT'S TIME TO ROCK!

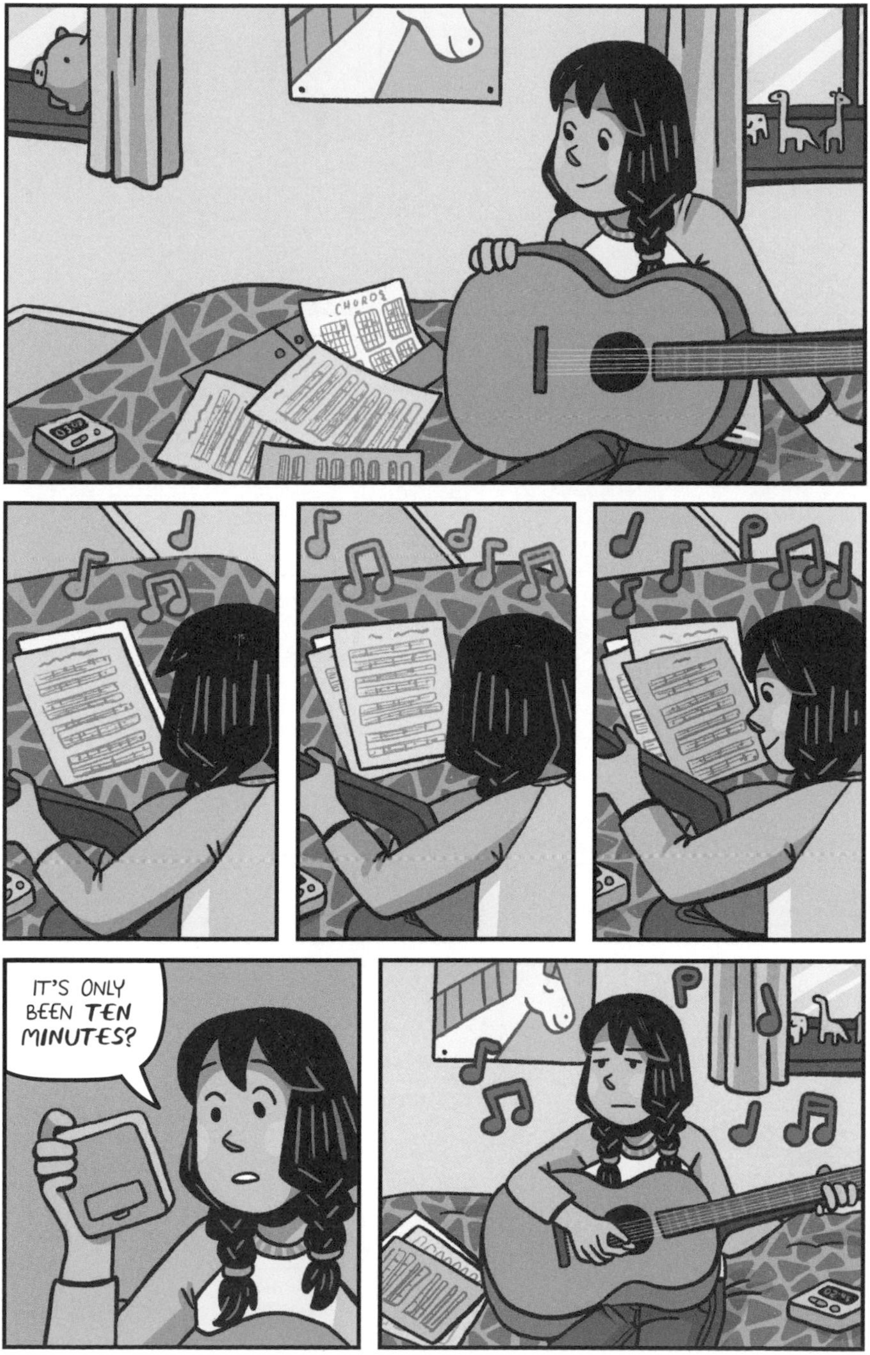
CHORDS
IT'S ONLY BEEN TEN MINUTES?

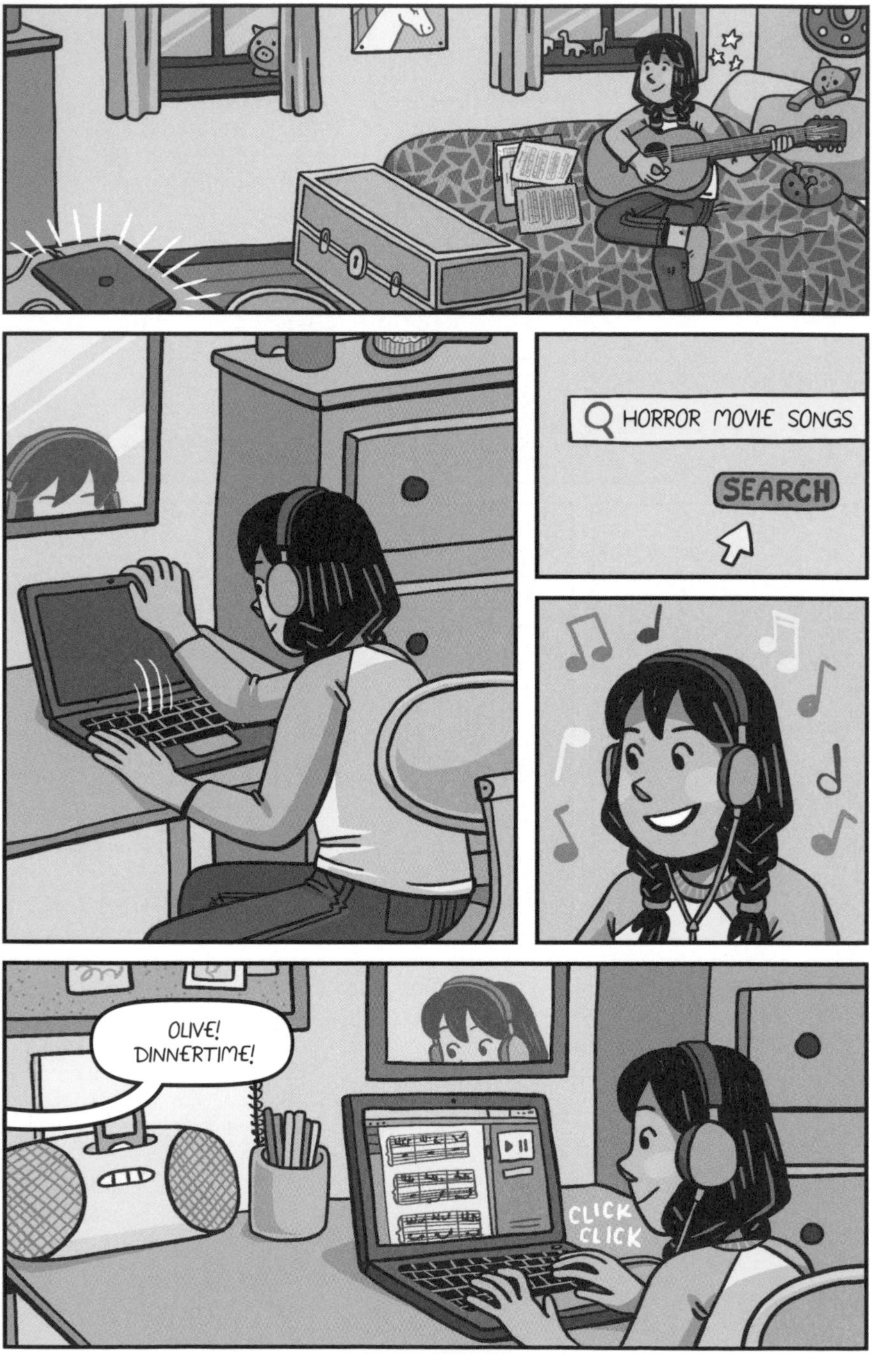
HORROR MOVIE SONGS
SEARCH
OLIVE! DINNERTIME!
CLICK CLICK

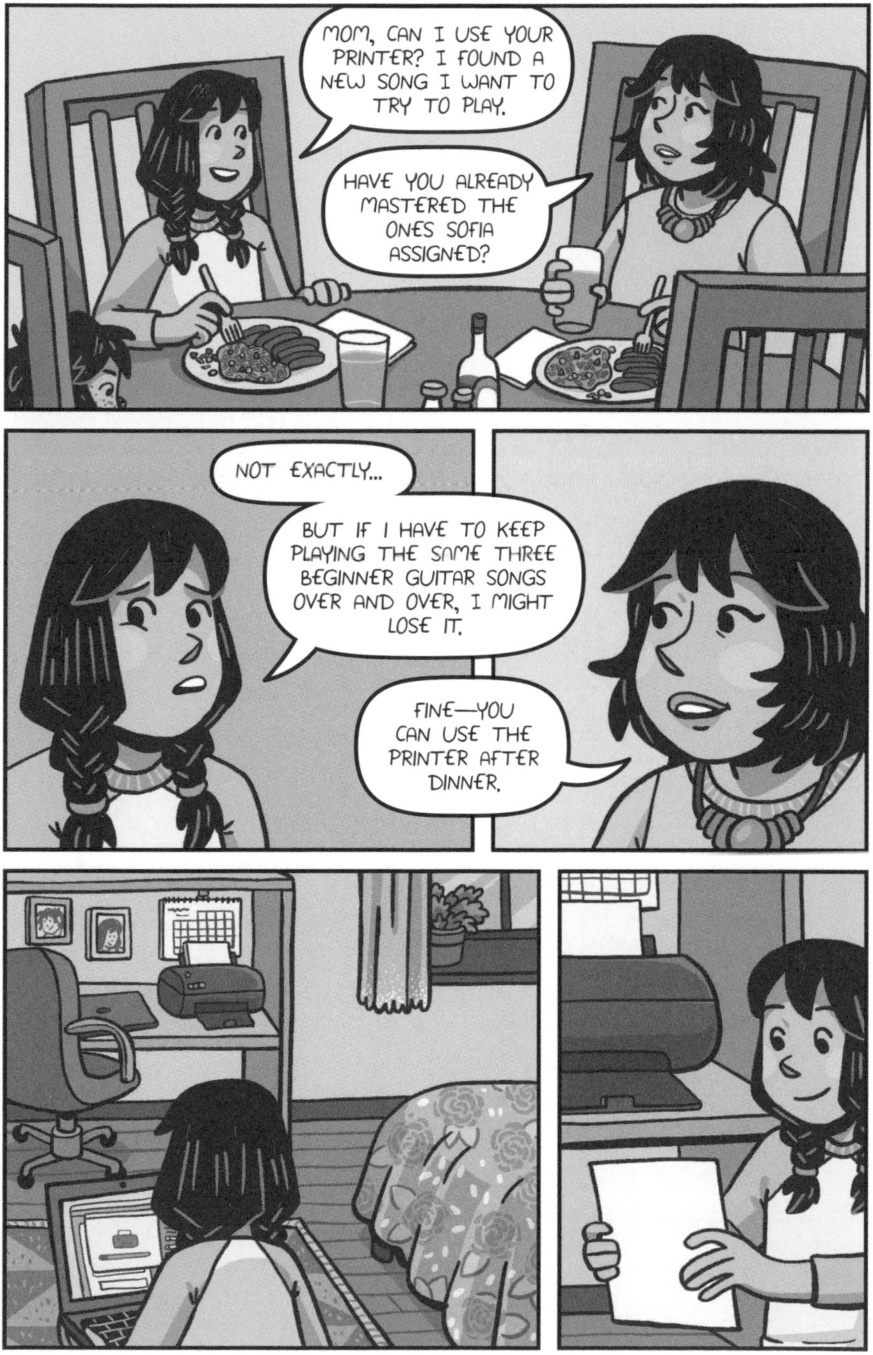
MOM, CAN I USE YOUR PRINTER? I FOUND A NEW SONG I WANT TO TRY TO PLAY.
HAVE YOU ALREADY MASTERED THE ONES SOFIA ASSIGNED?
NOT EXACTLY...
BUT IF I HAVE TO KEEP PLAYING THE SAME THREE BEGINNER GUITAR SONGS OVER AND OVER, I MIGHT LOSE IT.
FINE—YOU CAN USE THE PRINTER AFTER DINNER.

GUESS I HAVE TO FIGURE OUT THE TABS ON MY OWN...

WHAT WAS THAT?!

IF THAT'S HOW YOU SOUND WITH THREE HOURS OF PRACTICE A WEEK, MAYBE YOU NEED **30 HOURS** INSTEAD.

GET UP, HONEY.

TIME FOR SCHOOL.

BE SURE TO PUT EVERYTHING YOU NEED FOR YOUR GUITAR LESSON TOGETHER SO I CAN BRING IT WHEN I PICK YOU UP FROM THE BUS STOP.

YEAH...

OKAY.

HA HA

HA HA

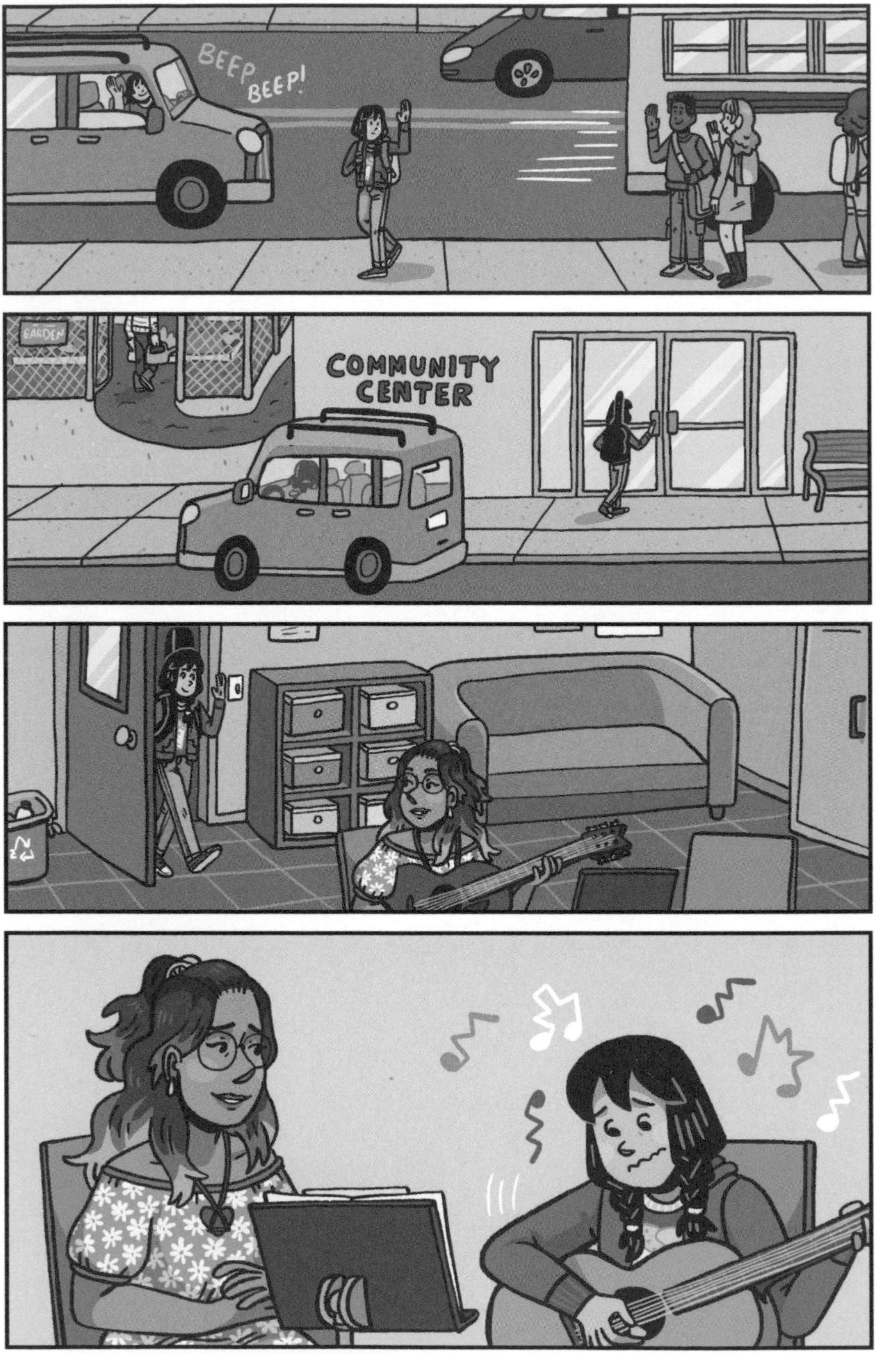
BEEP BEEP!
GARDEN
COMMUNITY CENTER

HAVE YOU BEEN PRACTICING?

YEAH! I PRACTICED FOR THREE WHOLE HOURS! YOU CAN ASK MY MOM AND BROTHER!

I BELIEVE YOU, OLIVE.

WE CAN KEEP WORKING ON THESE SONGS TOGETHER FOR AS LONG AS WE NEED TO.

SORRY, I DIDN'T MEAN TO INTERRUPT.

I'M OLIVE'S AUNT.

OH, IS OUR HOUR UP ALREADY? TIME GOT AWAY FROM ME.

I'M SOFIA.

MOLLY.

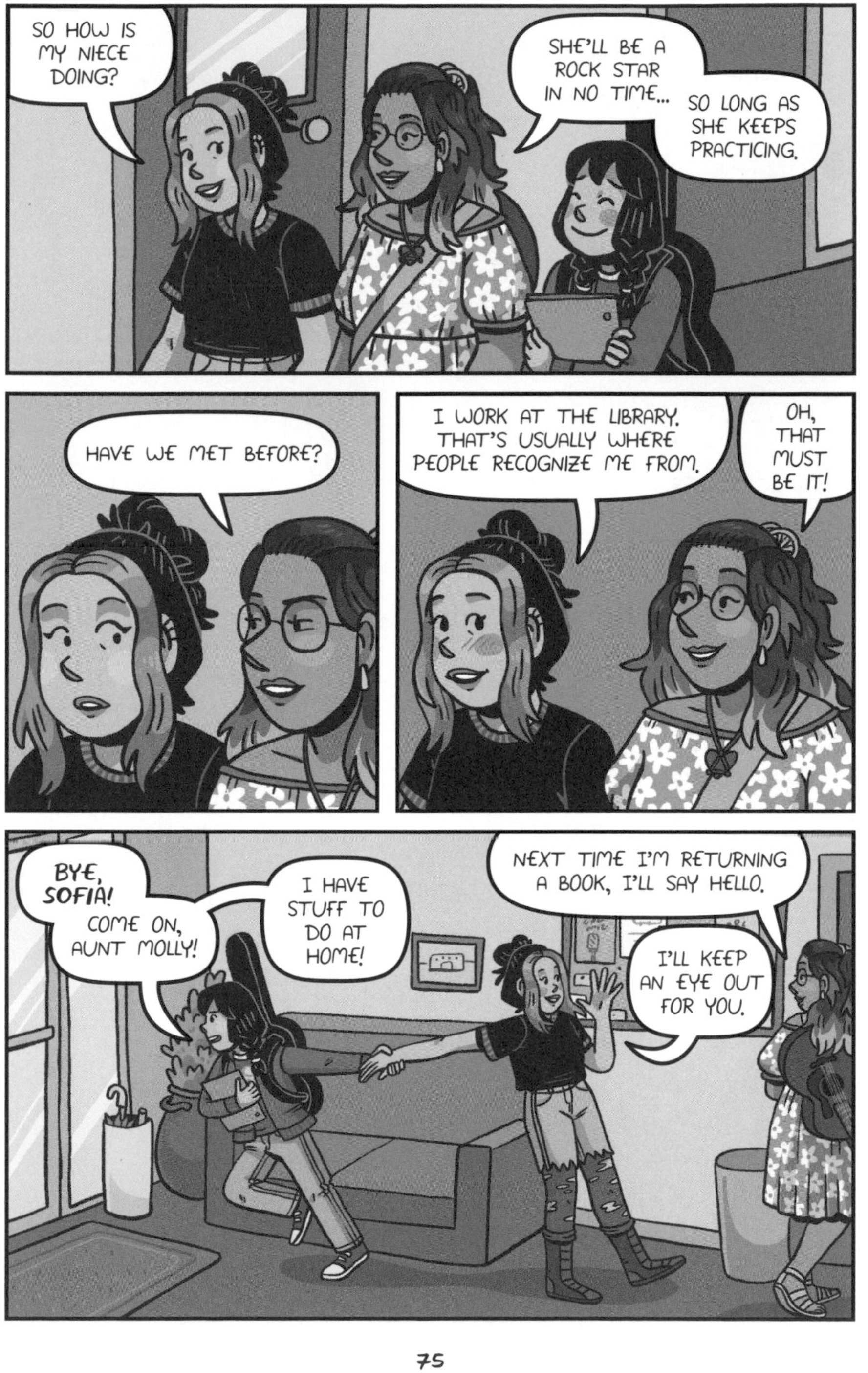
SO HOW IS MY NIECE DOING?
SHE'LL BE A ROCK STAR IN NO TIME...
SO LONG AS SHE KEEPS PRACTICING.
HAVE WE MET BEFORE?
I WORK AT THE LIBRARY. THAT'S USUALLY WHERE PEOPLE RECOGNIZE ME FROM.
OH, THAT MUST BE IT!
BYE, SOFIA!
COME ON, AUNT MOLLY!
I HAVE STUFF TO DO AT HOME!
NEXT TIME I'M RETURNING A BOOK, I'LL SAY HELLO.
I'LL KEEP AN EYE OUT FOR YOU.

ARE YOU READY?

WE'RE READY, SUGAR.

I PRESENT TO YOU—

MY MONSTER!

YOU DID A GREAT JOB SEWING, OLIVE, HONEY.

OH! YOU LOOK ADORABLE!

I'M NOT ADORABLE, *I'M FEROCIOUS!*

SMOOCH! SMOOCH!

STOP!

I'M VICIOUS!

COME ON, GOOB.

TIME TO CONSULT AN EXPERT.

RIIIIING RIIIIING

CALLING

BREE!

HEY, OLIVE...AND GOOBER-MONSTER?

WE NEED YOUR HELP. AS A COSTUME-CREATING COSPLAY QUEEN, WHAT WOULD YOU DO TO MAKE THIS COSTUME SCARY?

HMMM...

YOU COULD ADD BIGGER TEETH...

...OR MAYBE A BIGGER BROTHER?

SORRY, SIMON... BUT YOU'RE JUST TOO LITTLE AND CUTE.

IT'S HIS BLESSING AND HIS CURSE.

I GUESS WE CAN GIVE BIGGER TEETH A TRY AND HOPE FOR THE BEST.

GOOB, CAN YOU GET THE MODELING CLAY?

WHAT'S THE COSTUME FOR, ANYWAY?

I'M MAKING A MONSTER MOVIE!

THAT'S RAD! I CAN'T WAIT TO SEE IT!

WHAT ARE YOU UP TO?

RIGHT NOW?

TRYING TO FIGURE OUT WHAT TO DO FOR MY SCIENCE FAIR PROJECT.

I HAVE A FEW IDEAS...

WANT TO SHOW US?

WANT TO COME OVER THIS AFTERNOON?

I MADE YOU A COPY OF MY FIRST-AID NOTES—

WE COULD GO OVER THEM TOGETHER.

SORRY, WILLOW, I CAN'T. I HAVE STUDENT COUNCIL TODAY. HOW ABOUT TOMORROW?

OKAY.

OKAY, I THINK OLIVE AND TRENT HAD SOMETHING THEY WANTED TO SHARE?

WE ASKED A SAMPLE OF THE STUDENT BODY ABOUT THEIR EXPERIENCES WITH THE DRESS CODE...

...AND WE HAVE AN IDEA OF HOW WE'D LIKE TO SHARE THE INFORMATION WE GATHERED WITH YOU.

A DRESS CODE VIOLATION FASHION SHOW!

DRESS CODE VIOLATION FASHION SHOW

WE'D LIKE TO INVITE SOME OF THE KIDS WHO HAVE GOTTEN WARNINGS OR DETENTIONS TO COME TO ONE OF OUR MEETINGS WEARING THE OUTFITS THEY GOT IN TROUBLE FOR.

THAT WAY, YOU COULD SEE FIRSTHAND WHAT KIND OF CLOTHING IS GETTING CALLED OUT BY TEACHERS.

SO LONG AS THE KIDS CHANGE INTO THEIR OUTFITS FOR THE SHOW AFTER THE SCHOOL DAY ENDS, SINCE THE CLOTHES WOULD STILL BE AGAINST THE DRESS CODE AS IT CURRENTLY STANDS, AND THEY DON'T WEAR ANYTHING TOO OUTLANDISH...

...THAT SOUNDS LIKE A GREAT IDEA.

OPERATION FASHION SHOW IS A GO!

WHEN?

NEXT THURSDAY, AFTER SCHOOL.

BRING YOUR OUTFITS TO CHANGE INTO AFTER CLASS— LIV AND I WILL TAKE CARE OF THE REST.

CAN I STILL WALK THE RUNWAY IF I HAVEN'T HAD ANY RUN-INS WITH THE FASHION POLICE?

I CAN LOAN YOU SOME CLOTHES!

I'M A REPEAT DRESS-CODE OFFENDER.

AND I CAN FIND SOMETHING FOR YOU, EMILIE.

IS THERE ANYTHING I COULD DO TO HELP OUT? I AM TRENT'S OFFICIAL UNOFFICIAL VICE STUDENT COUNCIL REPRESENTATIVE, AFTER ALL.

OH, I'M SURE I CAN THROW TOGETHER AN OUTFIT FOR YOU, SAWYER.

HA HA HA HA HA HA HA

EVERYONE EMAIL ME YOUR LOOKS SO I CAN PLAN WHAT TO SAY DURING THE SHOW.

AND I'LL START WRITING AN INTRODUCTION.

TAKING THE LONG WAY HOME, OLIVE?

LAST TIME I CHECKED, YOU LIVED OVER THERE.

I'M GOING OVER TO WILLOW'S.

OH, COOL! I DIDN'T REALIZE WE WERE HANGING OUT TODAY!

UNLESS THIS IS JUST A WILLOW-AND-OLIVE-NO-HUGHS-ALLOWED THING.

YOU CAN COME, BUT WE'RE STUDYING FOR OUR BERRY SCOUT TEST...

YOU CAN LOOK OVER THE SCRIPT WHILE WE STUDY!

YOU FINISHED IT?

YEAH! *THIS* DRAFT, ANYWAY.

SO, IN THIS SCENE, IS THE SCIENTIST SCARED?

HE'S **SORT OF** SCARED BECAUSE OF THE MONSTER AND ALL...

...BUT HE'S MORE **DETERMINED.**

MAYBE WE SHOULD READ THROUGH IT TOGETHER.

YEAH!

WANNA TAKE A STUDY BREAK FOR ONE QUICK READ-THROUGH, WILLOW?

OKAY.

ACCORDING TO MY CALCULATIONS...

...THE MONSTER WILL DESTROY THE ENTIRE CITY BY SUNDOWN!

IT'S...UM...MY DUTY TO PROTECT THIS ISLAND... AND...UH...EVERYONE ON IT.

LET'S TRY THAT AGAIN, THIS TIME WITH A BIT MORE POWER.

REMEMBER, YOU'RE THE HERO!

SHOULD I SET TWO EXTRA PLACES FOR DINNER?

IS IT DINNERTIME ALREADY?

I TOLD MY MOM I'D BE HOME.

I'D BETTER HEAD OUT.

DON'T FORGET THESE!

DON'T WORRY. I'LL READ THESE TONIGHT AND WE'LL EARN THAT MERIT BADGE TOMORROW.

PIECE OF BERRY-FLAVORED CAKE!

LIV! CAN YOU HELP ME PRACTICE MY LINES?

HUH?

MY LINES FOR THE MOVIE!

YOU'RE PLAYING A MONSTER.

ALL OF YOUR LINES ARE "GRRRRR!"

I KNOW...BUT I WANT TO DO A GOOD JOB.

OKAY—I CAN STUDY LATER. SUIT UP AND GET GROWLING!

91

CLAP CLAP CLAP CLAP

DO YOU TWO KNOW WHAT TIME IT IS?

THIRTY MINUTES PAST *BEDTIME* FOR A CERTAIN LITTLE MONSTER.

MOM!

HEY, LIV,
I WAS TH—

NUH-UH.
I HAVE TO FOCUS.

PFFT!

Outfits I picked out for me and Chanda!
Lemme know if you need anything else.

OLIVE,

COME EAT SOME
LUNCH BEFORE YOUR
BERRY SCOUT MEETING.

I'LL BE
RIGHT
DOWN!

HONK!
HONK!

IS THAT MY RIDE ALREADY?

RIGHT ON TIME.

I NEED TO GET MY STUFF!

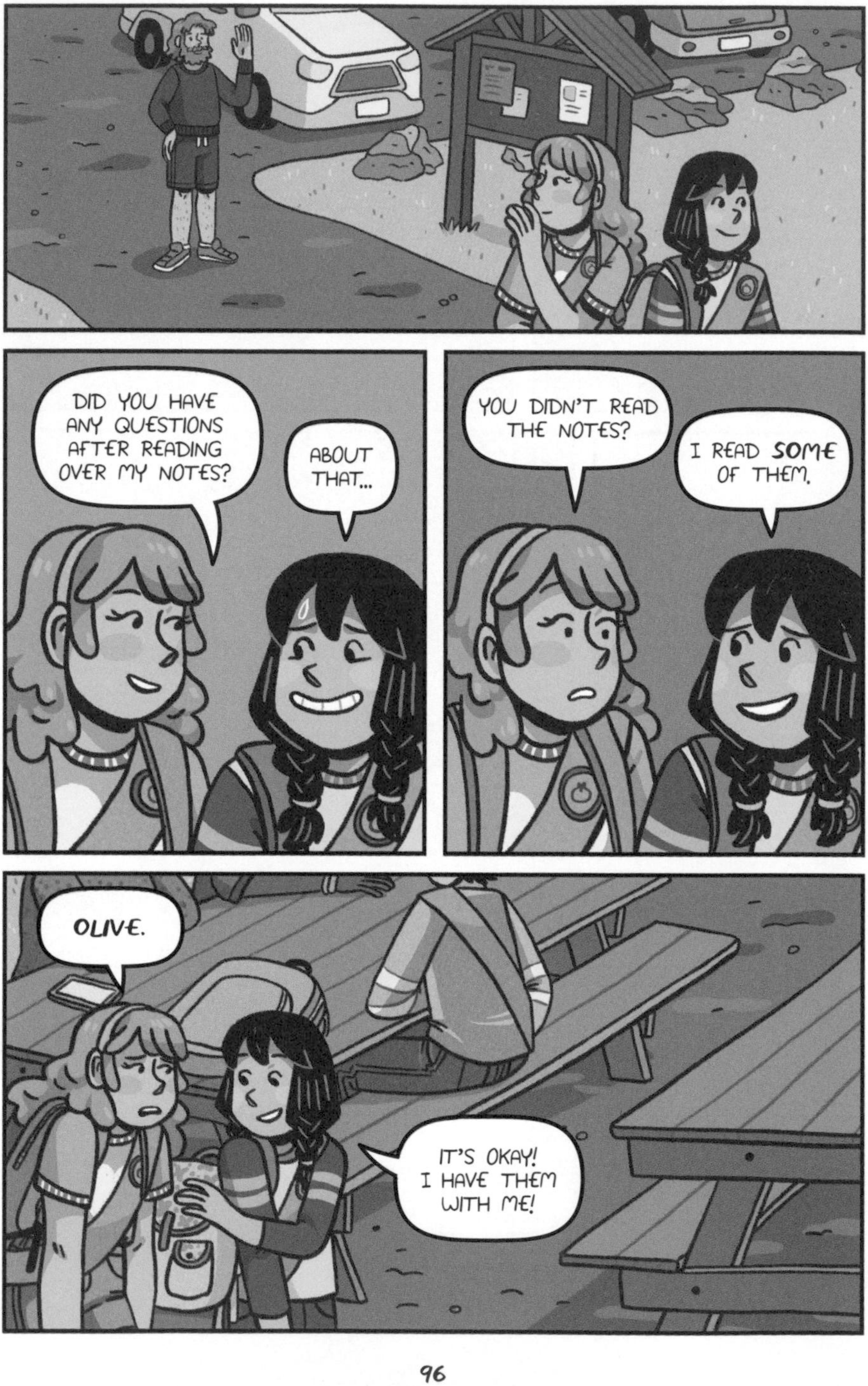
DID YOU HAVE ANY QUESTIONS AFTER READING OVER MY NOTES?
ABOUT THAT...
YOU DIDN'T READ THE NOTES?
I READ **SOME** OF THEM.
OLIVE.
IT'S OKAY! I HAVE THEM WITH ME!

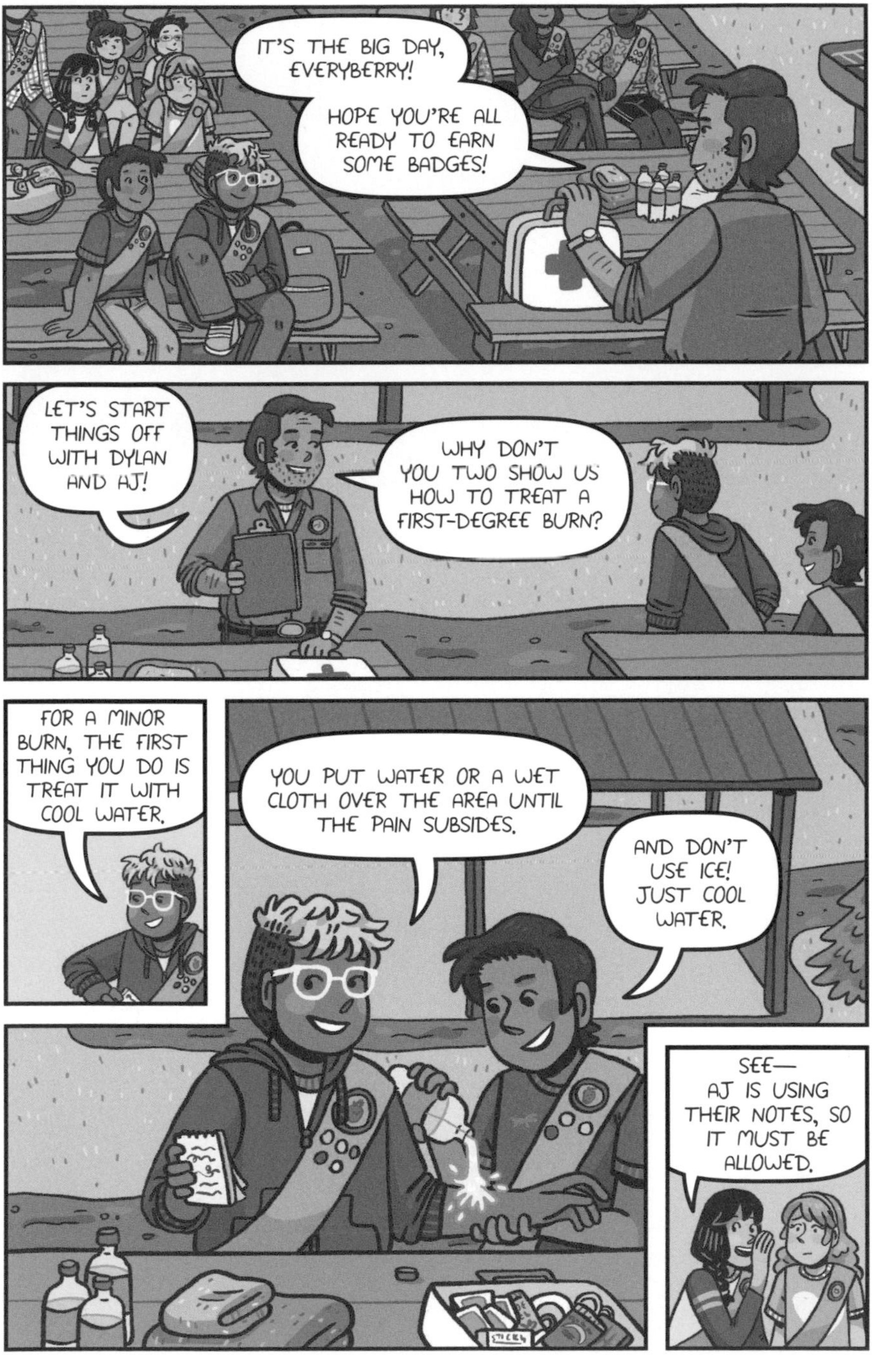
IT'S THE BIG DAY, EVERYBERRY!
HOPE YOU'RE ALL READY TO EARN SOME BADGES!
LET'S START THINGS OFF WITH DYLAN AND AJ!
WHY DON'T YOU TWO SHOW US HOW TO TREAT A FIRST-DEGREE BURN?
FOR A MINOR BURN, THE FIRST THING YOU DO IS TREAT IT WITH COOL WATER.
YOU PUT WATER OR A WET CLOTH OVER THE AREA UNTIL THE PAIN SUBSIDES.
AND DON'T USE ICE! JUST COOL WATER.
SEE— AJ IS USING THEIR NOTES, SO IT MUST BE ALLOWED.

ONCE IT'S CLEAN, YOU CAN PUT SOME ALOE VERA OR ANTIBIOTIC OINTMENT ON THE BURN—

DON'T USE BUTTER OR TOOTHPASTE OR ANY OTHER WEIRD HOME REMEDIES YOUR GRANDPA SWEARS BY.

THEN WRAP THE BURN IN GAUZE TO PROTECT IT WHILE IT HEALS. BE SURE TO CHANGE THE BANDAGE TWICE A DAY OR IT WILL GET GNARLY UNDER THERE.

GREAT JOB, YOU TWO! CONGRATS ON EARNING YOUR FIRST-AID MERIT BADGES!

ALL RIGHT. OLIVE AND WILLOW, YOU'RE UP!

SHOW US HOW TO TREAT AN ABRASION.

I DON'T HAVE
THE NOTES.

I MUST HAVE FORGOTTEN
THEM AT HOME.

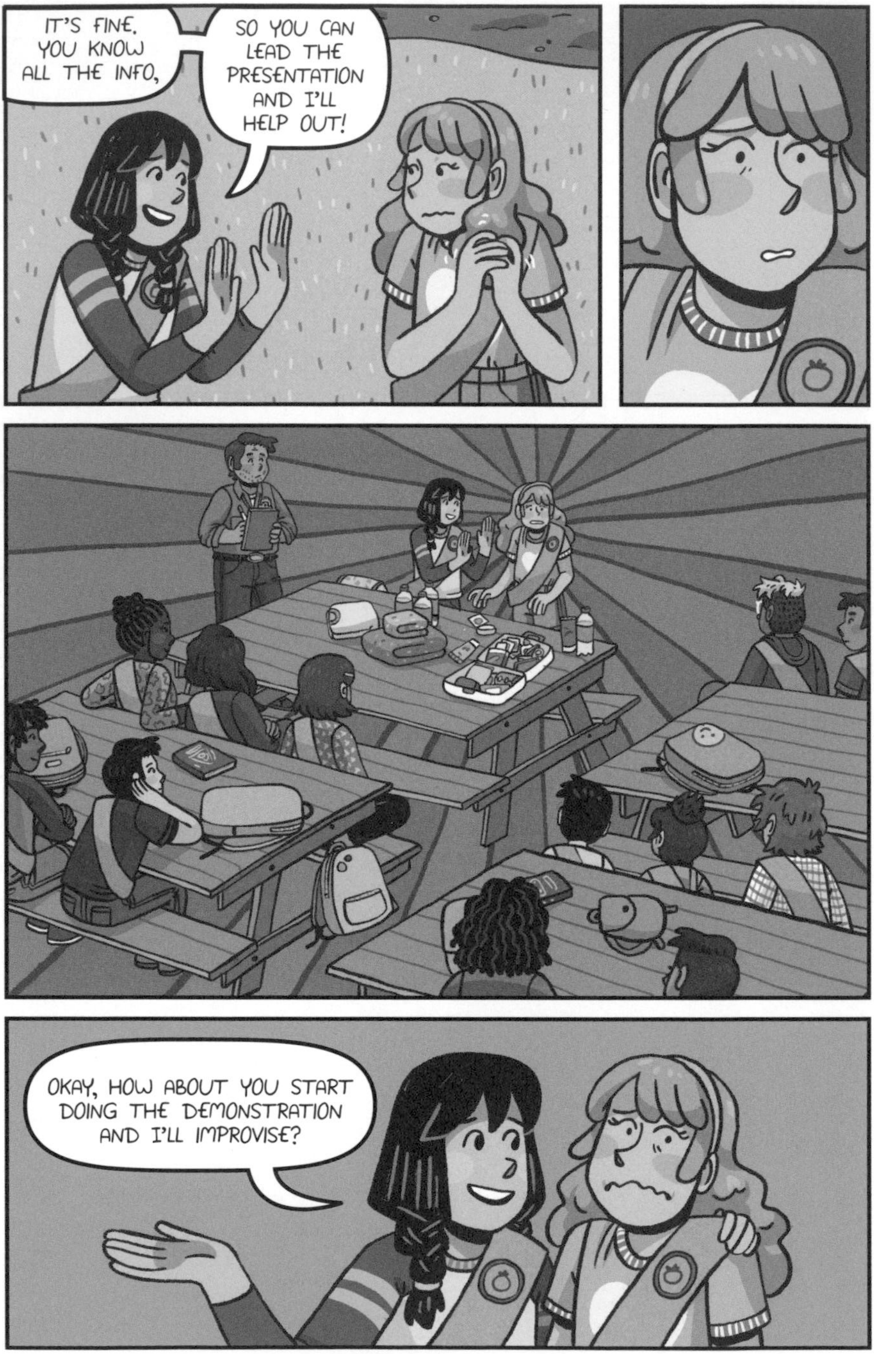
IT'S FINE. YOU KNOW ALL THE INFO,
SO YOU CAN LEAD THE PRESENTATION AND I'LL HELP OUT!
OKAY, HOW ABOUT YOU START DOING THE DEMONSTRATION AND I'LL IMPROVISE?

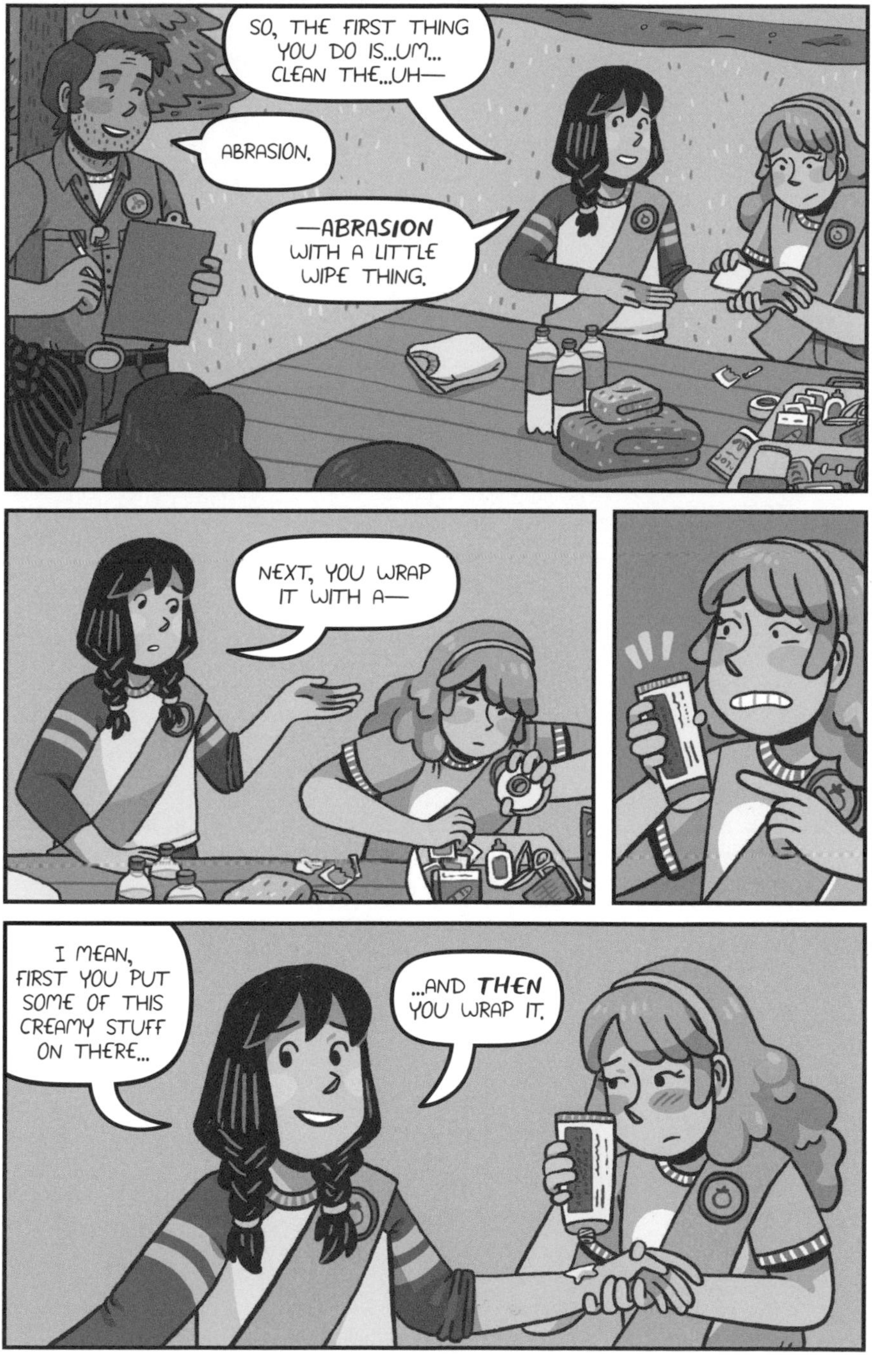

SO, THE FIRST THING YOU DO IS...UM... CLEAN THE...UH—
ABRASION.
—**ABRASION** WITH A LITTLE WIPE THING.
NEXT, YOU WRAP IT WITH A—
I MEAN, FIRST YOU PUT SOME OF THIS CREAMY STUFF ON THERE...
...AND **THEN** YOU WRAP IT.

THAT WAS A VALIANT EFFORT FOR A PAIR OF NEW BLUEBERRIES,

BUT I THINK YOU COULD DO WITH A LITTLE MORE PRACTICE.

I'M SURE YOU'LL GET YOUR FIRST-AID BADGE WHEN THE TEST ROLLS BACK AROUND NEXT YEAR.

ALL RIGHT, LET'S SEE HOW TO TREAT AN ALLERGIC REACTION FROM TARA AND ANTHONY.

HEY, WILLOW...

I'M REALLY SORRY WE DIDN'T GET OUR MERIT BADGES. I KNOW I SHOULD HAVE SPENT MORE TIME STUDYING YOUR NOTES. I HOPE YOU'RE NOT **BERRY** MAD AT ME?

GIRLS! READY TO HEAD OUT?

IT'S OKAY.

IT'S NOT LIKE I DID A **BERRY** GOOD JOB EITHER.

DO YOU STILL WANT TO COME OVER AND WORK ON THE MOVIE TOMORROW?

SURE.

SWEETHEART, YOUR FRIENDS ARE HERE!

AND... ACTION.

ACCORDING TO MY CALCULATIONS...

...THAT MONSTER WILL DESTROY THE ENTIRE CITY BY SUNDOWN.

WE...

UM...

WE HAVE TO DO SOMETHING...

CUT.

THAT WAS... GOOD.

BUT... DO YOU THINK YOU COULD READ THAT LINE WITH A BIT MORE CONVICTION, WILLOW?

YOUR CHARACTER IS THE **HERO,** SO YOU HAVE TO BE CONFIDENT AND TAKE CHARGE, OKAY?

I'LL TRY.

ACTION!

WE HAVE TO **DO...** SOMETHING?

OKAY, CUT.

LET'S TRY IT AGAIN.

BEEP

WAS THAT TAKE STILL BAD?

I'M SORRY I'M NOT GOOD AT THIS.

I'M TRYING...

I KNOW.

I CAN TELL YOU'RE TRYING...

HOW ABOUT WE SWITCH THINGS UP A LITTLE?

I'LL PLAY THE PART AND YOU CAN WORK THE CAMERA.

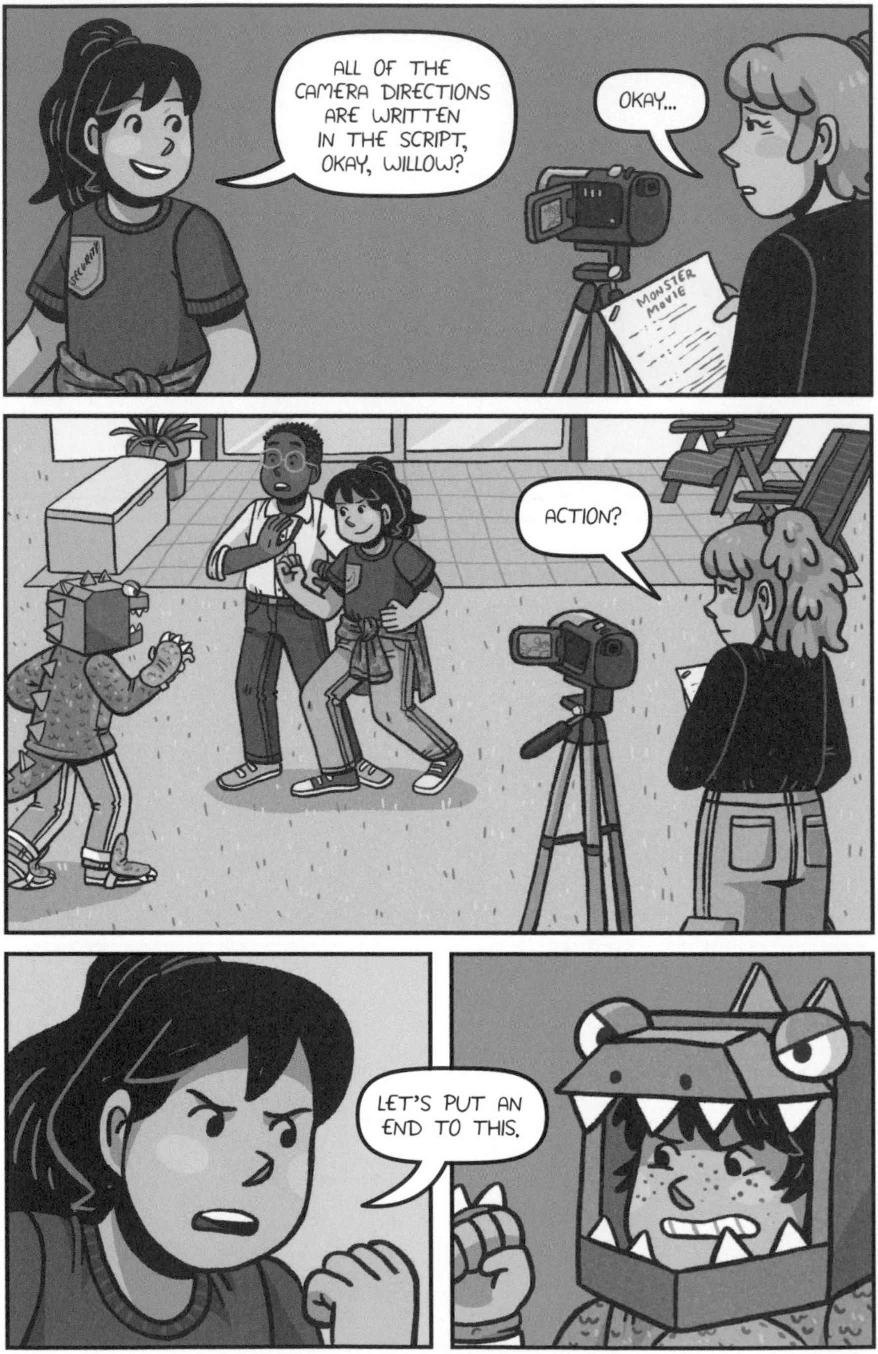
ALL OF THE CAMERA DIRECTIONS ARE WRITTEN IN THE SCRIPT, OKAY, WILLOW?
OKAY...
MONSTER MOVIE
ACTION?
LET'S PUT AN END TO THIS.

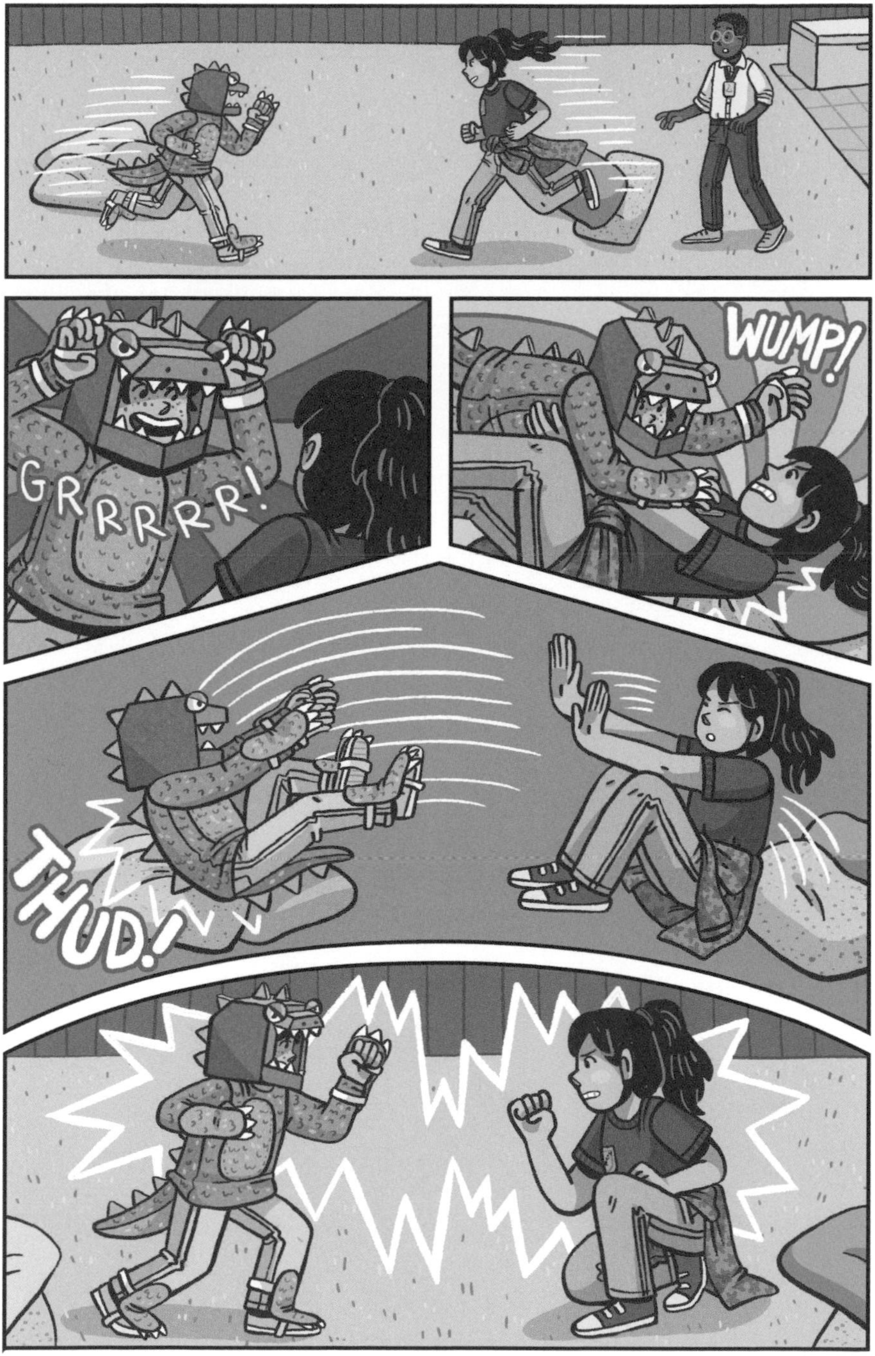
GRRRRRR!
WUMP!
THUD!

REWIND AND LET'S SEE HOW IT LOOKS.

UH, OKAY.

YOU WERE SUPPOSED TO PAN OVER TO THE RIGHT AND THEN ZOOM IN...

HUGH ISN'T EVEN IN FRAME...

IT'S OKAY. I CAN FIX EVERYTHING IN POST.

DON'T WORRY!

WHY DO YOU KEEP LOOKING INTO THE CAMERA?

I WAS TRYING TO SEE IF WILLOW WAS ZOOMING.

SHE WASN'T ZOOMING.

KIDS! DINNER!

DINNER ALREADY?

AND I HAVEN'T EVEN STARTED MY HOMEWORK YET.

SO, HOW IS YESTERDAY'S FOOTAGE LOOKING?

IT'S LOOKING GOOD! A LOT OF...

GOOD STUFF IN THERE.

HEY, OLIVE!

OH, HEY, AVA.

THANKS FOR EMAILING ME THOSE PICTURES.

NO PROBLEM.

I STILL NEED TO KNOW WHAT EVERYONE ELSE WILL BE WEARING.

WE'LL EMAIL YOU TONIGHT— RIGHT, NAT?

YEAH, SURE.

WHAT'S UP, LIV?

CAN'T TALK.

I WANT TO FINISH THE HOMEWORK MRS. GRIFFIN ASSIGNED THIS MORNING **NOW**, SO I'LL HAVE LESS TO DO AFTER SCHOOL.

SHRUG.

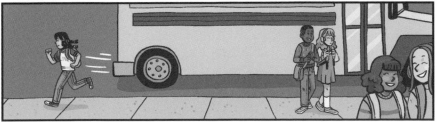

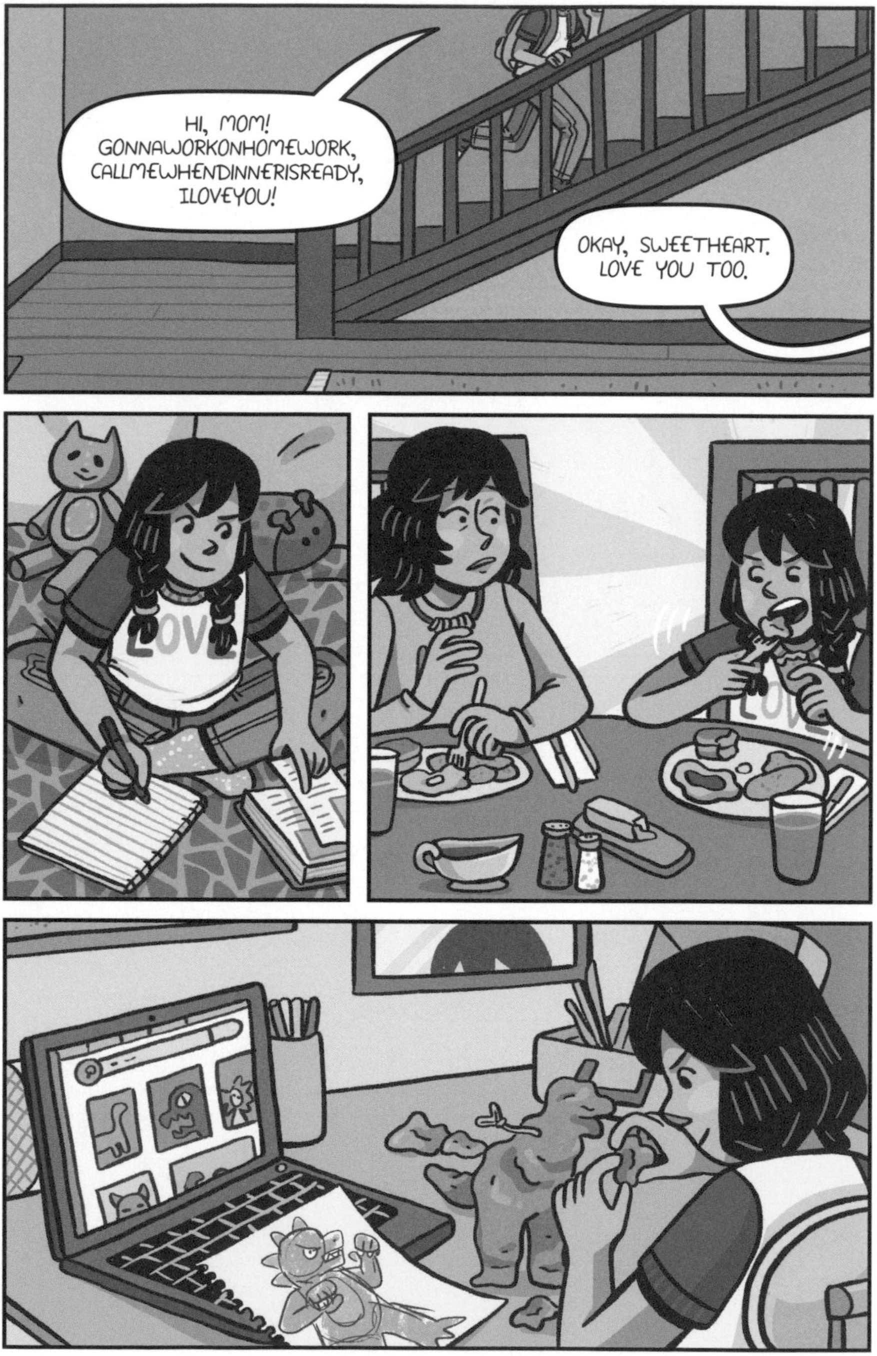
HI, MOM! GONNAWORKONHOMEWORK, CALLMEWHENDINNERISREADY, ILOVEYOU!
OKAY, SWEETHEART. LOVE YOU TOO.
LOVE
LOVE

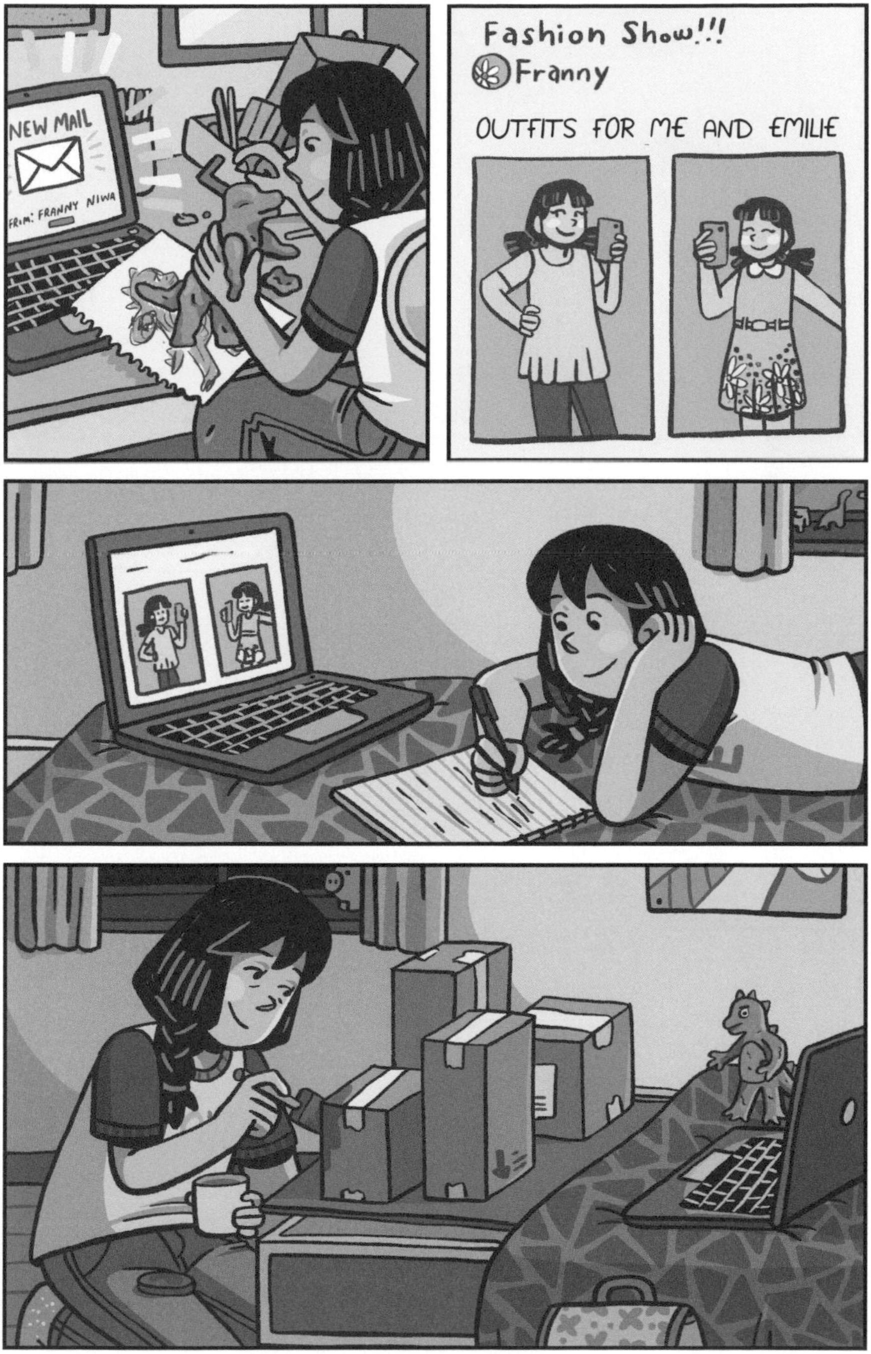
NEW MAIL
FROM: FRANNY NIWA
Fashion Show!!!
Franny
OUTFITS FOR ME AND EMILIE

OLIVE? ARE YOU NOT UP YET?

GET A MOVE ON!

WHAT'S FOR BREAKFAST?

BANANA NUT MUFFIN—

TO GO!

HURRY OR YOU'RE GOING TO MISS YOUR BUS.

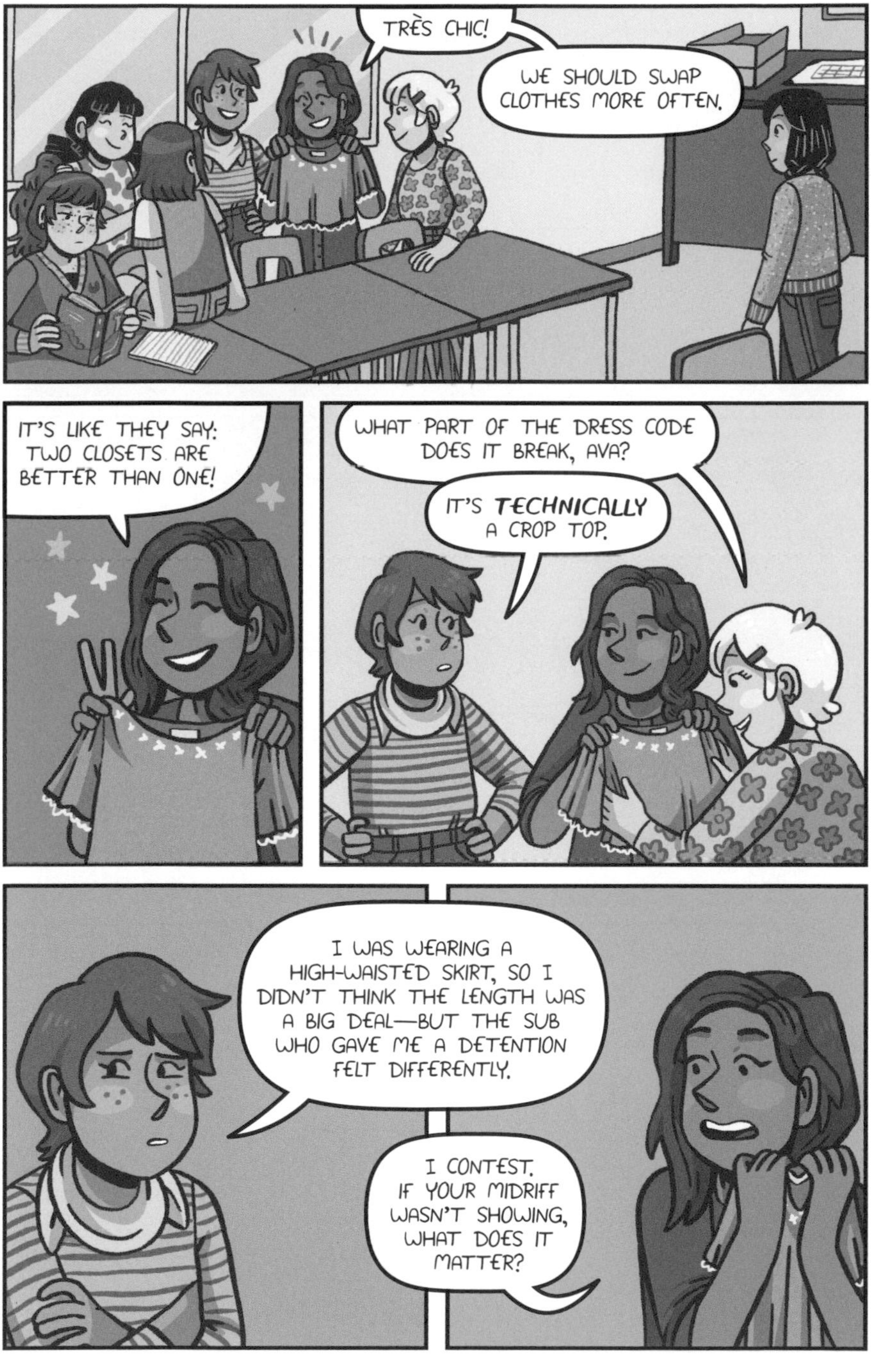
TRÈS CHIC!
WE SHOULD SWAP CLOTHES MORE OFTEN.
IT'S LIKE THEY SAY: TWO CLOSETS ARE BETTER THAN ONE!
WHAT PART OF THE DRESS CODE DOES IT BREAK, AVA?
IT'S **TECHNICALLY** A CROP TOP.
I WAS WEARING A HIGH-WAISTED SKIRT, SO I DIDN'T THINK THE LENGTH WAS A BIG DEAL—BUT THE SUB WHO GAVE ME A DETENTION FELT DIFFERENTLY.
I CONTEST. IF YOUR MIDRIFF WASN'T SHOWING, WHAT DOES IT MATTER?

I HAVE THE DRESS I PICKED OUT FOR YOU ON A HANGER IN MY LOCKER.

YAY!

THAT REMINDS ME...

YOU STILL NEED TO TELL ME WHAT YOU AND SAWYER ARE GOING TO WEAR, NAT.

YEAH, YEAH... I'LL EMAIL YOU.

HEY, LIV!

PRE-LUNCHROOM MUNCHING, HUH?

INNOVATIVE! I LOVE IT.

I'M NOT GOING TO LUNCH TODAY. I HAVE SOME RESEARCH I WANT TO DO IN THE LIBRARY.

ARE WE ALLOWED TO DO THAT?

I GUESS I'LL FIND OUT IF SOMEONE STOPS ME.

SEE YA LATER!

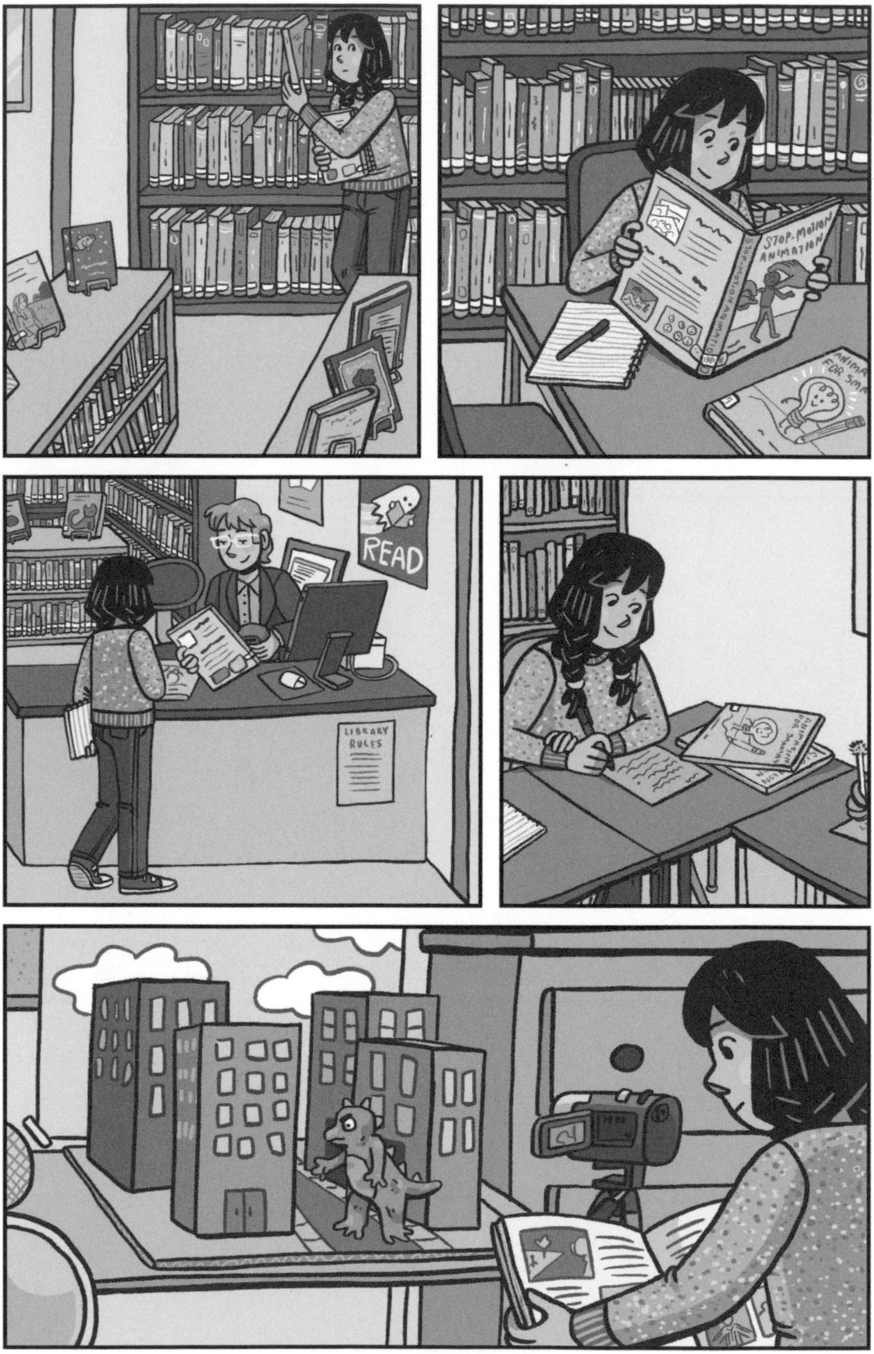
STOP-MOTION ANIMATION
READ
LIBRARY RULES

OLIVE! DINNER!

DO YOU REMEMBER WHAT TOMORROW IS?

UMM...

...IS IT...

...GRANDMA'S BIRTHDAY?

YOUR GRANDMA'S BIRTHDAY IS IN JULY. YOU HAVE A GUITAR LESSON TOMORROW.

I COMPLETELY FORGOT.

I CAN PRACTICE FOR THREE HOURS AFTER I FINISH EATING.

I KNOW LAST TIME WE TALKED ABOUT THIS, I WAS AGAINST YOU QUITTING GUITAR...

BUT IT SEEMS LIKE YOU'RE SPREADING YOURSELF SO THIN LATELY.

IF YOU WANTED TO PUT YOUR MUSIC LESSONS ON HOLD FOR A LITTLE WHILE, WE COU—

NO!

I REALLY WANT TO LEARN GUITAR!

I'VE GOT EVERYTHING UNDER CONTROL, I CAN HANDLE IT!

ALL RIGHT, SWEETHEART.

IS THAT THE SONG YOU WANT TO PUT IN THE MOVIE?

YEAH.

IT DOESN'T SOUND VERY GOOD.

I STILL HAVE MORE THAN A WEEK TO GET THE HANG OF IT BEFORE THE FILM SUBMISSIONS ARE DUE.

IS THAT THE STOP-MOTION SCENE? CAN I SEE?

I GUESS.

IS IT *SUPPOSED* TO LOOK SILLY?

DON'T YOU HAVE YOUR OWN ROOM TO HANG OUT IN?

I JUST CALL 'EM LIKE I SEE 'EM!

NAT,

YOU HAVEN'T SENT ME THAT EMAIL YET.

THE FASHION SHOW ISN'T UNTIL TOMORROW AFTER SCHOOL. YOU REALLY NEED TO CHILL OUT.

GETTING A HEAD START ON HOMEWORK AGAIN, LIV?

NO... I FORGOT TO DO MY MATH HOMEWORK LAST NIGHT.

YIKES. WE'LL LEAVE YOU TO IT, THEN...

GOOD LUCK! IF IT'S THE SAME ASSIGNMENT WE HAD, YOU'LL NEED IT.

COMMUNITY CENTER

IT'S OKAY. LET'S GO THROUGH THE SONG A BIT SLOWER TO SEE WHERE YOU'RE GETTING STUCK.

HEY, SOFIA?

YES?

IF SOMEONE WANTED TO, COULD THEY RECORD A SONG ON THEIR LAPTOP?

YEAH—
THERE ARE FREE MUSIC-EDITING PROGRAMS, AND MOST COMPUTERS HAVE SOME SORT OF MIC.

BUT YOU HAVE A LITTLE WAYS TO GO BEFORE YOU RELEASE YOUR FIRST SINGLE, NO?

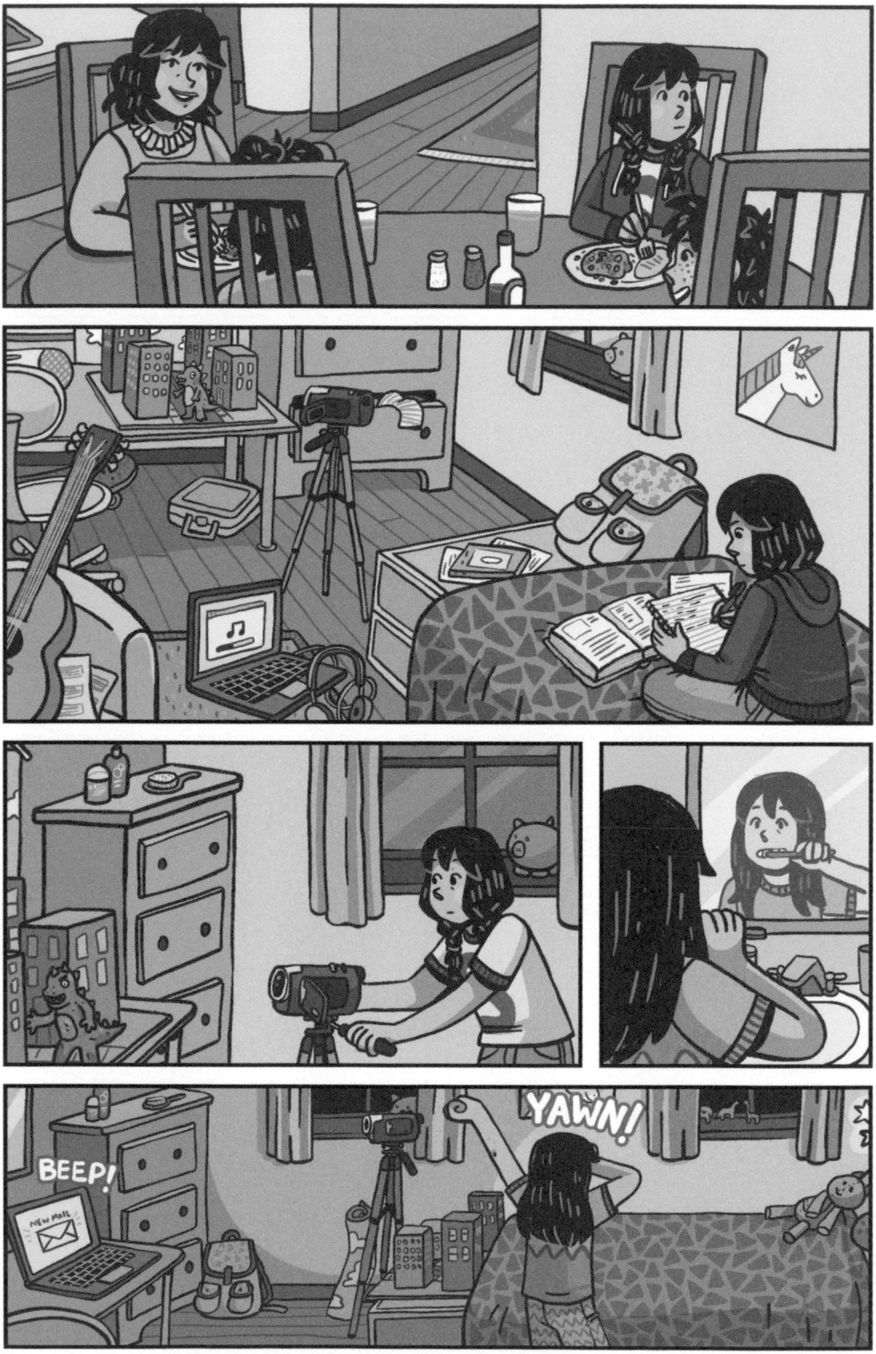
YAWN!
BEEP!
NEW MAIL

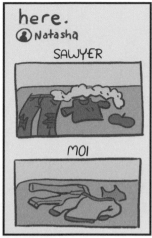

here.
🔘 Natasha

SAWYER

MOI

• • •

WHAT ARE YOU DOING UP?

I JUST HAVE TO FINISH THIS ONE THING BEFORE BED. IT'S FOR STUDENT COUNCIL.

OKAY...BUT DON'T TAKE TOO MUCH LONGER— IT'S LATE.

OH, GOOD, YOU'RE HERE.

NOW WE CAN START FILMING.

WAIT—

WHO ARE YOU?!

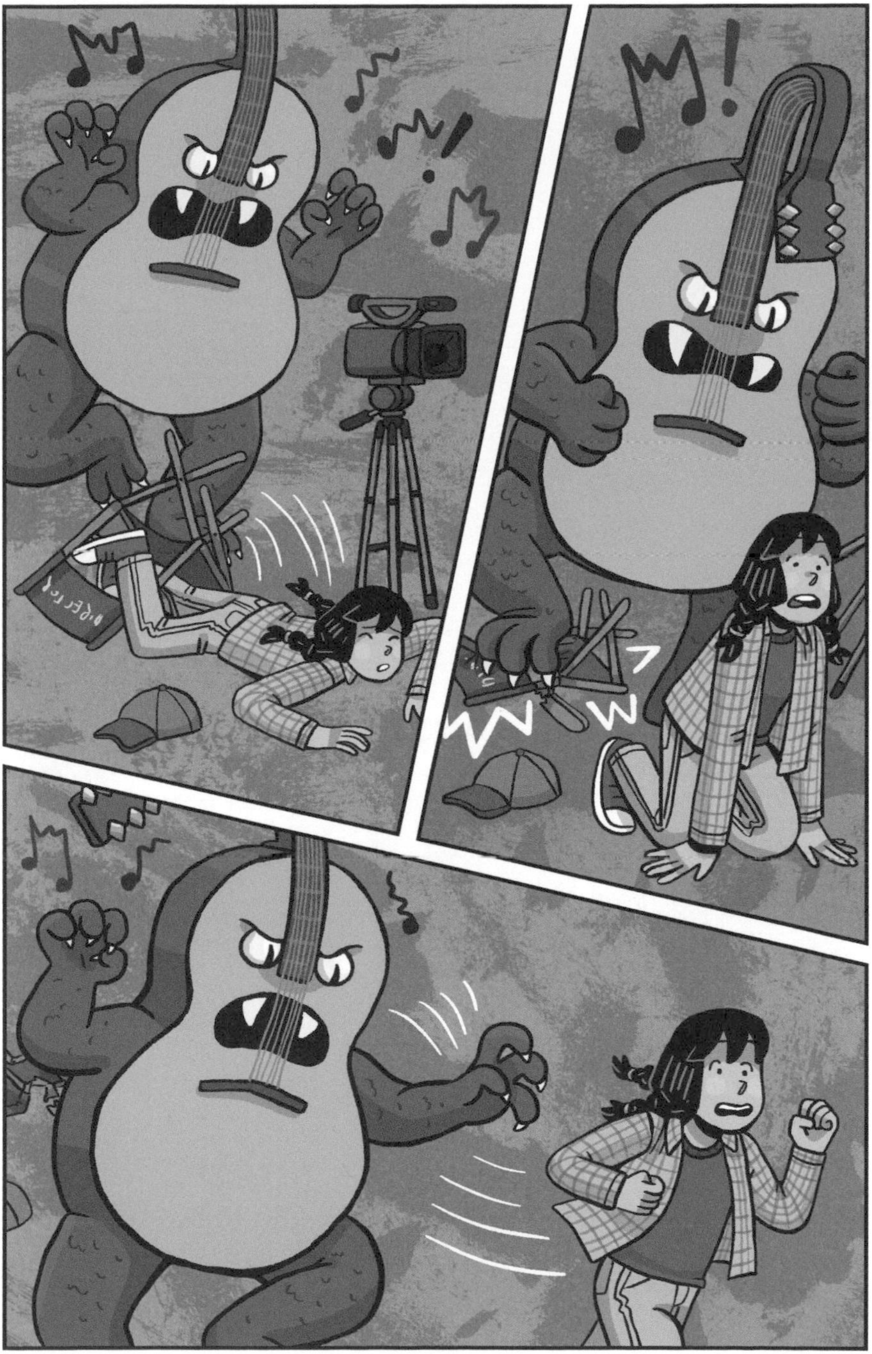

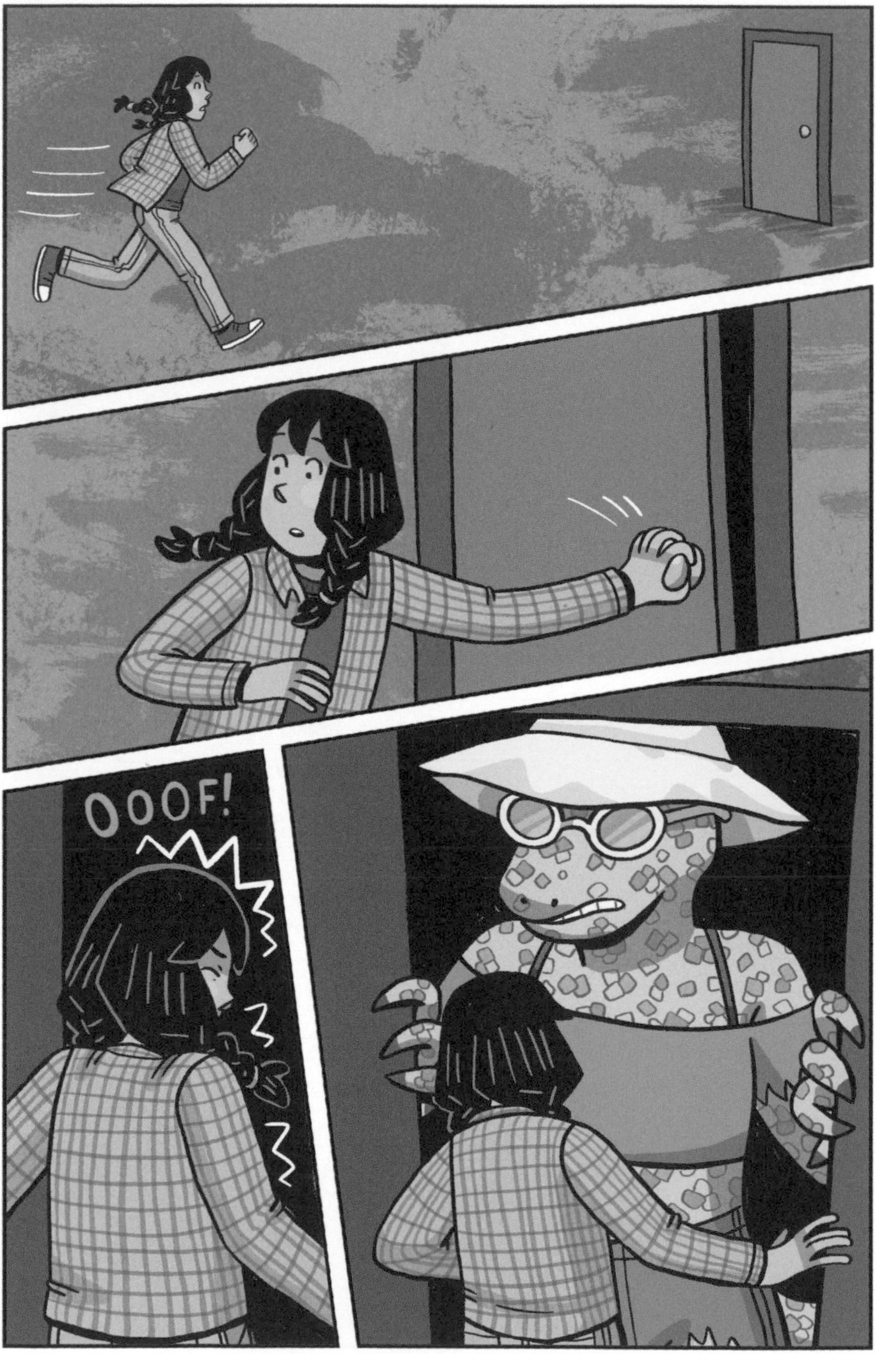
OOOF!

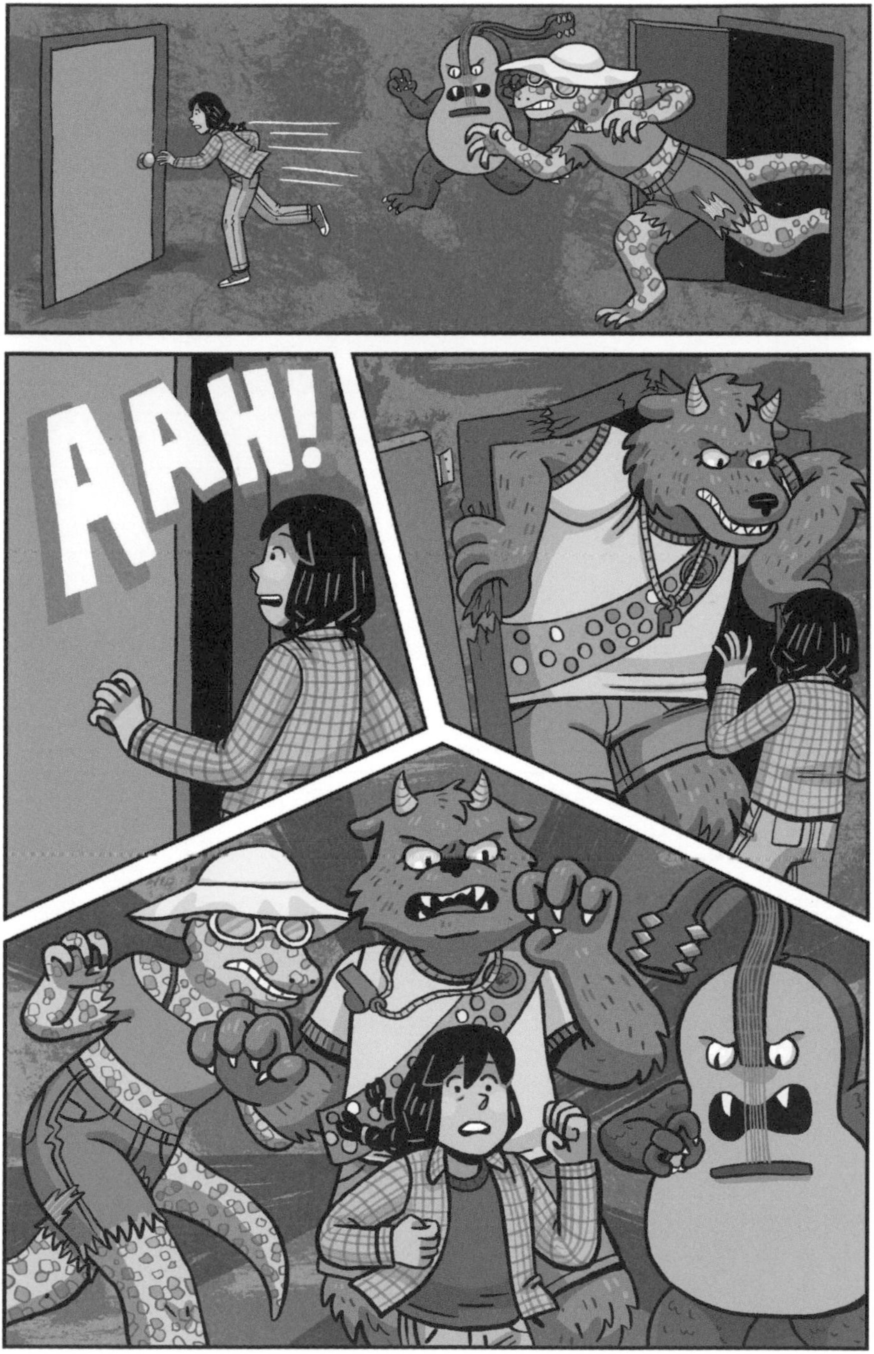
AAH!

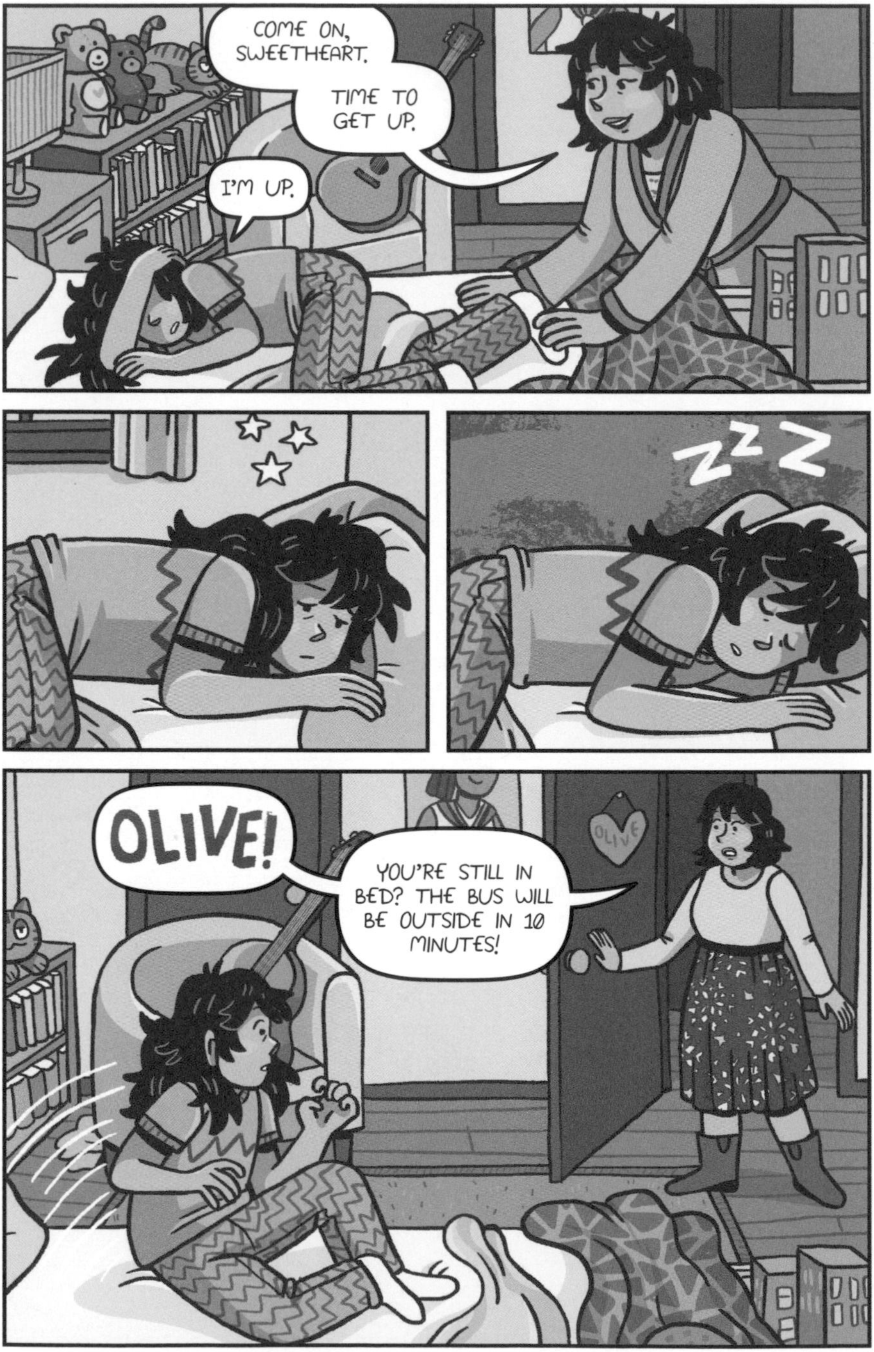
COME ON, SWEETHEART.
TIME TO GET UP.
I'M UP.
OLIVE!
YOU'RE STILL IN BED? THE BUS WILL BE OUTSIDE IN 10 MINUTES!

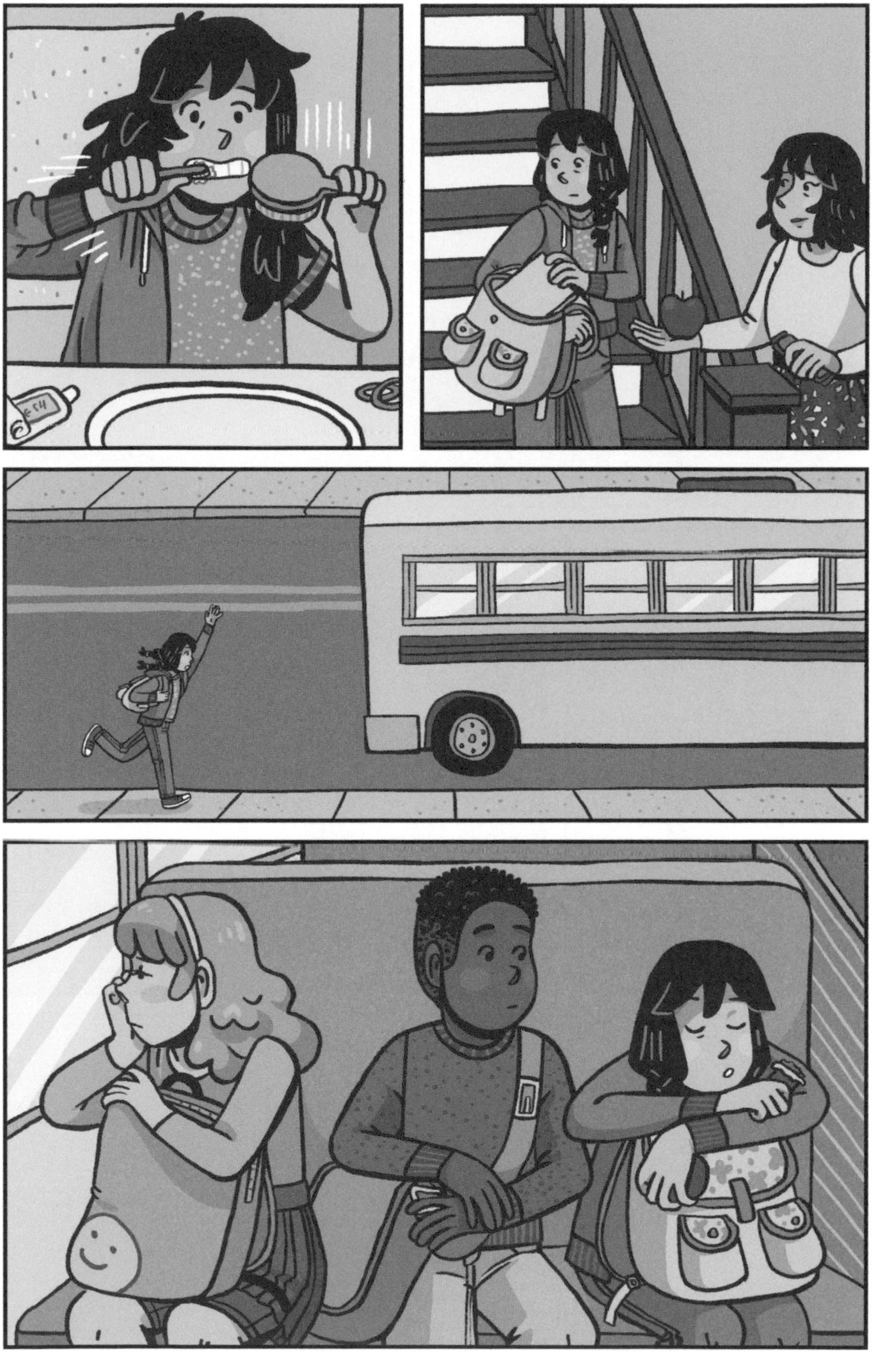

SO...DID YOU GET MY EMAIL, OLIVE?

YES, THANK YOU FOR BEING SO **PROMPT.**

I DO WHAT I CAN.

DID YOU REMEMBER TO BRING EXTRA CLOTHES FOR ME?

OF COURSE— THEY'RE IN MY LOCKER.

YOU'RE GOING TO LOOK **FABULOUS!**

WHY DOES THAT SOUND LIKE A THREAT?

HEY, LIV. ARE YOU BUSY?

FOR ONCE, NO.

DO YOU WANT TO READ OVER THE INTRO I WROTE FOR THE FASHION SHOW?

SURE, AND YOU CAN READ OVER MY JOKES.

THIS PRESENTATION IS GOING TO BE SO GOOD.

YEAH.

HEH

HOPEFULLY GOOD ENOUGH TO CONVINCE MS. LIN TO CHANGE THE DRESS CODE.

CLASS, TODAY WE HAVE A SPECIAL TREAT: IT'S MOVIE TIME!

AND I EVEN MADE POPCORN.

WHAT IS AN ELECTRON? LET'S GET A CLOSER LOOK...

ALL RIGHT! I'LL SEE YOU ALL TOMORROW.

HERE YOU GO, SAWYER.

C'MON, WE CAN CHANGE IN THE GYM LOCKER ROOMS.

YOU READY, PARTNER?

I WANT TO GO OVER MY NOTES ONE MORE TIME. I'LL BE THERE IN A SECOND.

OKAY.

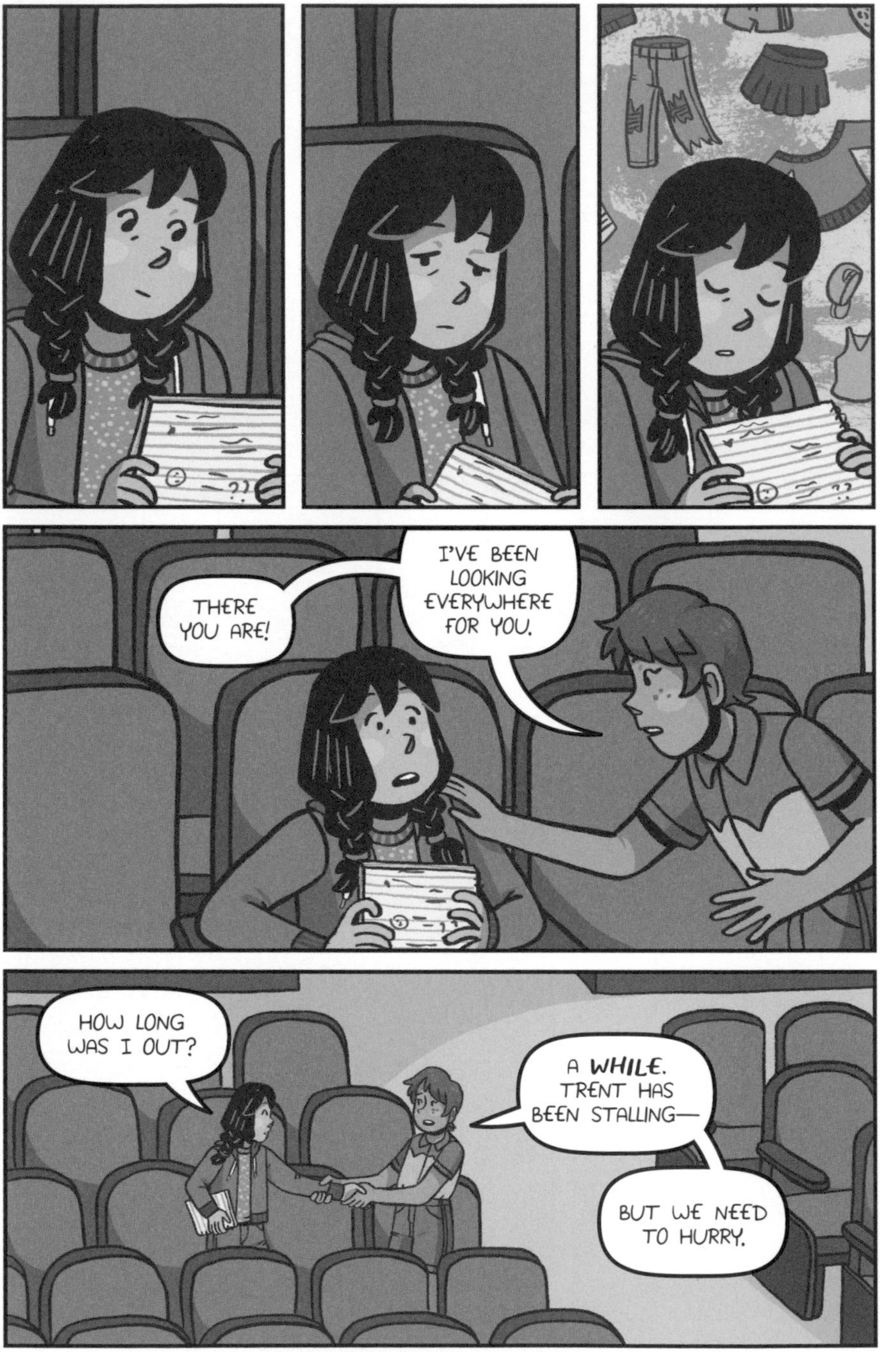
THERE YOU ARE!
I'VE BEEN LOOKING EVERYWHERE FOR YOU.
HOW LONG WAS I OUT?
A WHILE. TRENT HAS BEEN STALLING—
BUT WE NEED TO HURRY.

IS SOMETHING WRONG?

ARE YOU OKAY, LIV?

EVERYTHING'S FINE.

...AND IF WE CALL SHORT PANTS "SHORTS," WHY DON'T WE CALL LONG PANTS "LONGS"?

GET IN THERE.

UH, HEY!

IT SEEMS LIKE THIS INTRODUCTION IS RUNNING A LITTLE **LONG**, AM I RIGHT?

LET'S GET THIS FASHION SHOW ON THE ROAD!

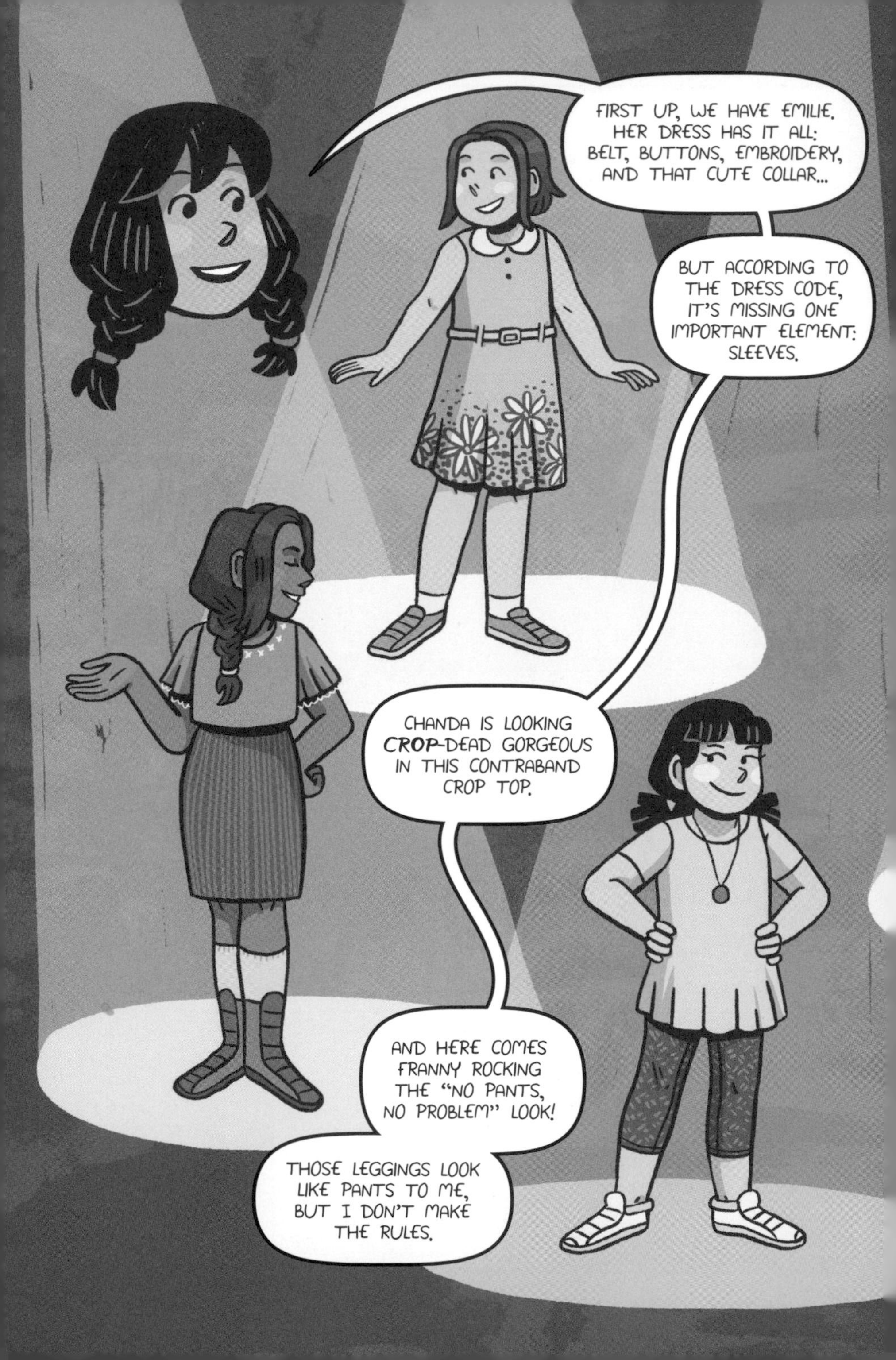
FIRST UP, WE HAVE EMILIE. HER DRESS HAS IT ALL: BELT, BUTTONS, EMBROIDERY, AND THAT CUTE COLLAR...
BUT ACCORDING TO THE DRESS CODE, IT'S MISSING ONE IMPORTANT ELEMENT: SLEEVES.
CHANDA IS LOOKING **CROP**-DEAD GORGEOUS IN THIS CONTRABAND CROP TOP.
AND HERE COMES FRANNY ROCKING THE "NO PANTS, NO PROBLEM" LOOK!
THOSE LEGGINGS LOOK LIKE PANTS TO ME, BUT I DON'T MAKE THE RULES.

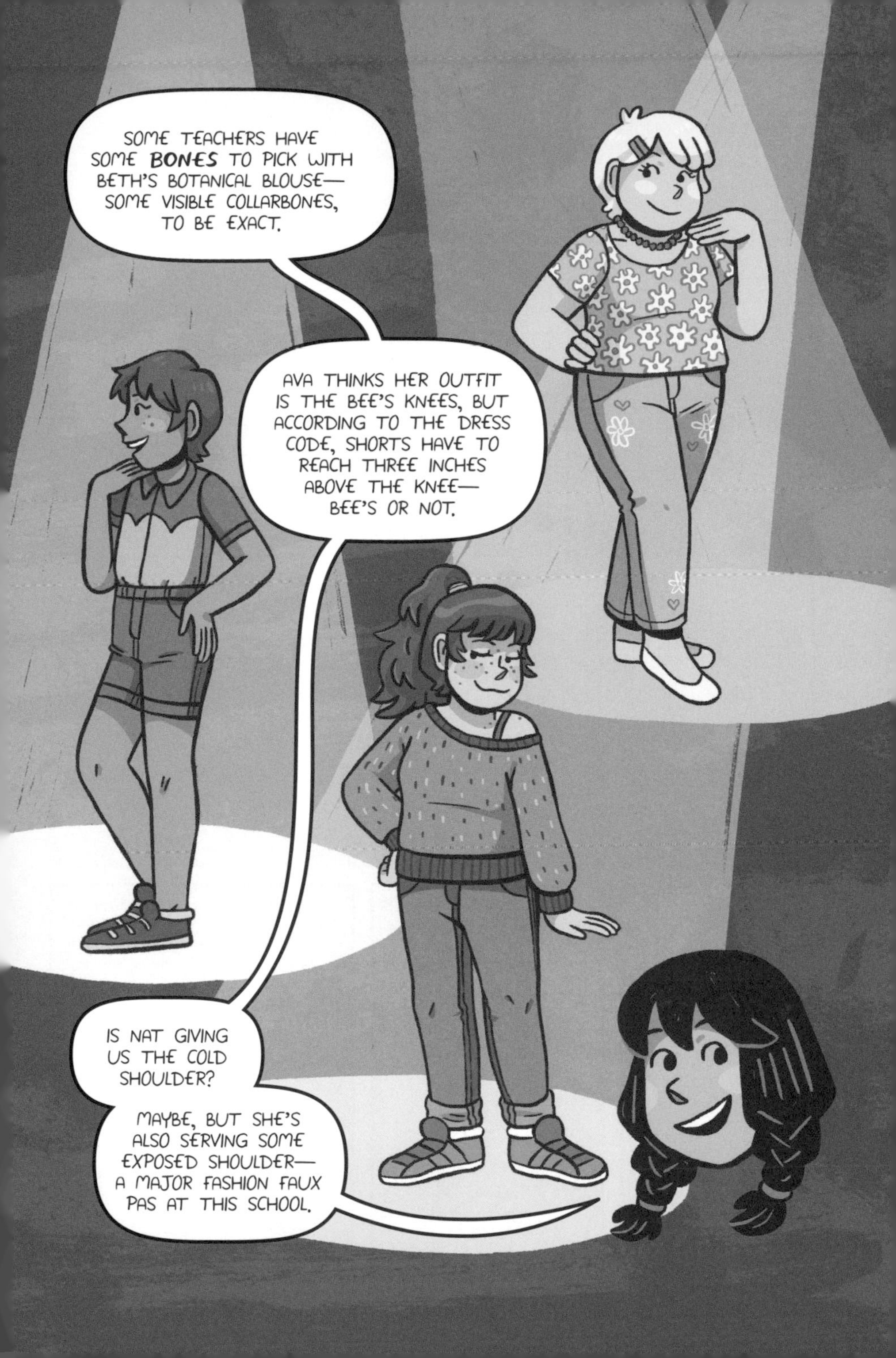
SOME TEACHERS HAVE SOME **BONES** TO PICK WITH BETH'S BOTANICAL BLOUSE— SOME VISIBLE COLLARBONES, TO BE EXACT.
AVA THINKS HER OUTFIT IS THE BEE'S KNEES, BUT ACCORDING TO THE DRESS CODE, SHORTS HAVE TO REACH THREE INCHES ABOVE THE KNEE— BEE'S OR NOT.
IS NAT GIVING US THE COLD SHOULDER?
MAYBE, BUT SHE'S ALSO SERVING SOME EXPOSED SHOULDER— A MAJOR FASHION FAUX PAS AT THIS SCHOOL.

AND FINALLY, A *LOOK* THAT WOULD LEAVE THE FASHION POLICE SPEECHLESS...

SAWYER'S SPORTING RIPPED JEANS, BARE SHOULDERS, SUNGLASSES, **AND** A HAT INDOORS.

HOW MANY DETENTIONS IS THAT?

THAT WAS CERTAINLY ILLUMINATING... AND ENTERTAINING.

I DON'T SEE ANY REASON WHY YOU SHOULDN'T BE ALLOWED TO WEAR THESE CLOTHES TO SCHOOL.

WITH THE EXCEPTION OF SOME OF MR. MOORE'S ACCESSORIES, I THINK IT'S ABOUT TIME WE UPDATED OUR RULES A LITTLE.

SO, WHAT WAS THAT VANISHING ACT ABOUT? WHERE DID YOU GO?

I...SORT OF FELL ASLEEP.

YOU FELL ASLEEP AT SCHOOL?

ARE YOU FEELING OKAY?

IT'S NOT LIKE YOU TO SNEAK IN A NAP RIGHT BEFORE SHOWTIME.

YEAH, ESPECIALLY AFTER YOU PUT SO MUCH WORK INTO IT.

I'M JUST **TIRED**.

DO YOU WANT TO TALK ABOUT IT?

I THOUGHT I COULD DO EVERYTHING I WANTED TO IF I JUST TRIED **REALLY** HARD...BUT MAYBE I TOOK ON TOO MUCH.

SORRY ABOUT TODAY.

HEY, YOU DID FINE... ONCE YOU SHOWED UP.

IS THERE ANYTHING I CAN HELP YOU WITH?

YOU REALLY WANT TO HELP?

REALLY.

COUNT ME IN, TOO!

YEAH! YOU'RE ALWAYS HELPING EVERYONE ELSE— LET US HELP YOU!

WELL, THE FASHION SHOW IS OVER... AND YOU CAN'T REALLY HELP ME WITH BERRY SCOUTS OR MY MUSIC LESSONS, BUT I COULD USE A FEW EXTRA HANDS FOR MY MOVIE.

WHAT'S IT ABOUT?

MOVIE?

I'M TRYING TO MAKE A SHORT ABOUT A MONSTER TO ENTER IN THE FILM FESTIVAL AT THE COMMUNITY CENTER.

LET'S HANG OUT TOMORROW AFTER SCHOOL. YOU CAN FILL US IN ON THE DETAILS.

BUT WE'RE SUPPOSED TO GO TO THE SKATE PARK TOMORROW!

THEN LET'S MEET UP AT THE SKATE PARK.

MY BROTHER'S GIRLFRIEND GAVE ME HER OLD ROLLER SKATES AND I'VE BEEN LOOKING FOR AN EXCUSE TO TRY THEM OUT.

I WAS THINKING, MAYBE YOU SHOULD GO TO BED EARLY TONI—

GOOD NIGHT, SWEETHEART.

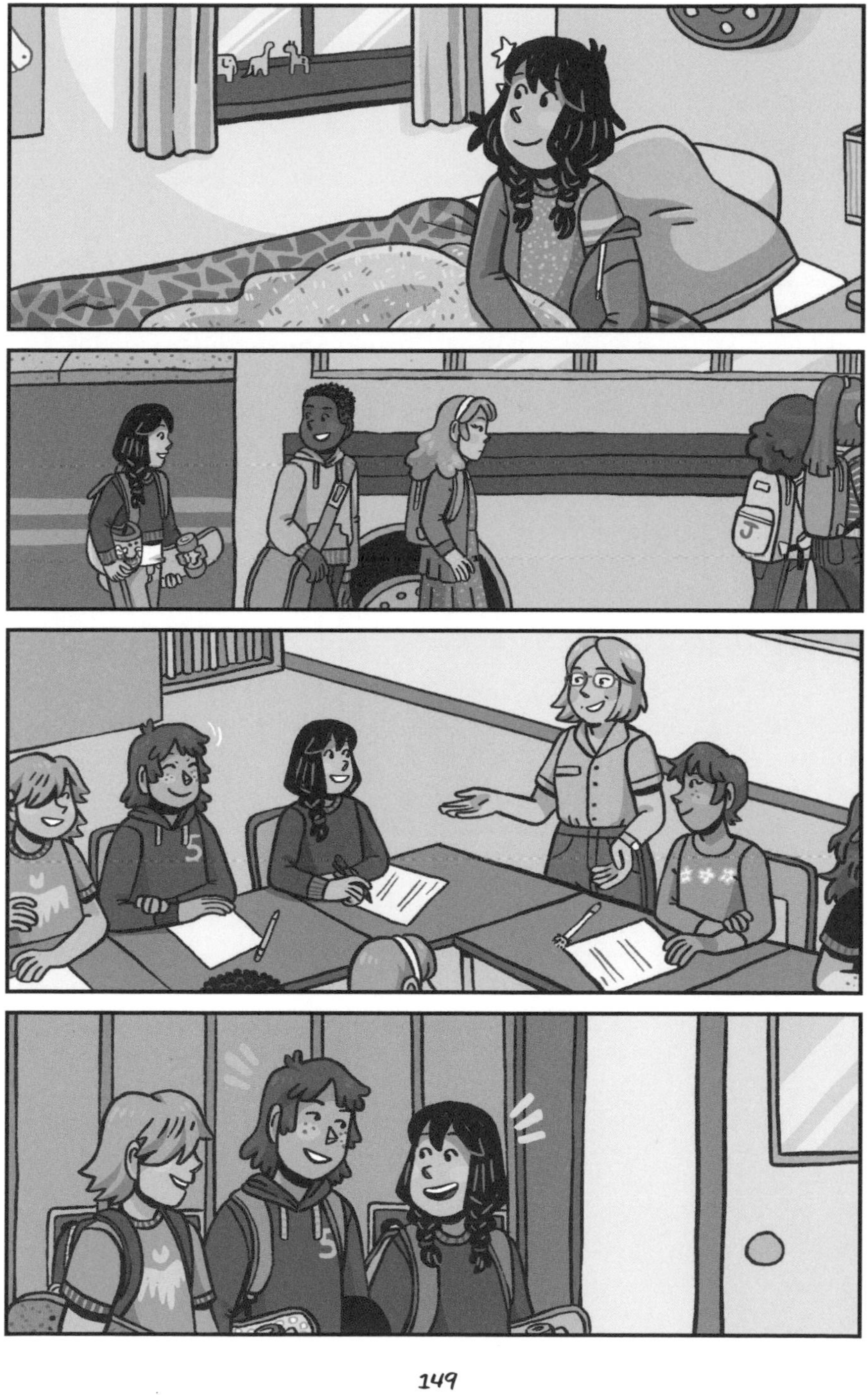

OLIVE! RIDE IN MARC'S NEW—ER, TECHNICALLY USED— CAR WITH US!

UMM...

YOU SHOULD RIDE WITH US, LIV. CAM HAS BEEN ASKING ABOUT YOU EVER SINCE YOU CAME OVER.

MAYBE NEXT TIME, AVA! I WANT TO SAY HI TO TRENT'S LITTLE SISTER!

I SHOULD HAVE WARNED YOU ABOUT CONVERTIBLES AND LONG HAIR...

HA HA HA HA

RAWR!

SORRY. I DIDN'T MEAN TO LAUGH...

IT'S OKAY. IT *IS* SORT OF FUNNY.

IT MUST BE HARD TO MAKE SOMETHING *ACTUALLY* SCARY.

THINK ABOUT ALL THE BIG-BUDGET HORROR MOVIES THAT END UP BEING FUNNY WHEN THEY'RE TRYING TO BE SERIOUS.

TRYING TO BE SERIOUS...

WHAT IF INSTEAD OF TRYING TO BE **SERIOUS**, WE TRIED TO BE **FUNNY**?

IT'S ALREADY A LITTLE GOOFY, SO MAYBE WE SHOULD LEAN INTO THAT.

IF WE REIMAGINE THE MOVIE AS A COMEDY, THE LOW PRODUCTION VALUES AND SILLY COSTUMES COULD WORK IN OUR FAVOR!

THAT'S A GREAT IDEA!

OKAY. I'M DONE ROLLER-SKATING FOR THE DAY...

MAYBE FOREVER. I'LL WATCH YOUR STUFF IF YOU WANT TO SKATEBOARD.

I'M HOME.

HELLO, SWEETHEART.

BREE CALLED WHILE YOU WERE OUT.

SHE WANTS TO SHOW YOU SOMETHING.

I TOLD HER YOU COULD VIDEO-CHAT AFTER DINNER.

THANKS, MOM.

RIIIIING!

CALLING

OLLIE!

BUMBLE-BREE!

WHAT WAS THE THING YOU WANTED TO SHOW ME?

OH YEAH! IT'S A VIDEO FROM THE SCIENCE FAIR...

HOLD ON, I'M GOING TO SCREEN-SHARE.

WHOA!

HOW DID YOU DO THAT?

BAKING SODA, VINEGAR, AND FOOD COLORING... PLUS SOME DRY ICE AND LED LIGHTS FOR DRAMATIC EFFECT!

AND I MADE THE BACK OF THE VOLCANO A CUTAWAY USING A PANEL OF PLEXIGLASS SO YOU CAN SEE THE INNER WORKINGS.

YOU REALLY IMPROVED UPON A CLASSIC!

WOULD YOU LET ME USE THAT ERUPTION FOOTAGE IN MY MOVIE?

GO RIGHT AHEAD.

YOU'RE IN A GOOD MOOD TODAY. ARE THINGS LOOKING UP WITH YOUR MOVIE?

DEFINITELY.

BUT THAT'S THE ONLY THING LOOKING UP...

...I SORT OF MESSED THINGS UP WITH WILLOW...AGAIN. I WAS SUPPOSED TO HELP HER WITH THIS PRESENTATION FOR BERRY SCOUTS, BUT I KEPT PUTTING OFF PRACTICING AND THEN I FORGOT MY NOTES AND...

BASICALLY WE DIDN'T EARN OUR MERIT BADGES.

MERIT BADGES? ARE THOSE A BIG DEAL?

NOT TO ME, BUT WILLOW'S UPSET.

I GUESS I CAN MAKE IT UP TO HER BY TRYING HARDER TO EARN THE NEXT BADGE— BUT BERRY SCOUTS JUST ISN'T MY THING.

AND IT'S FRUSTRATING BECAUSE SHE KNEW THE INFORMATION AND TOTALLY COULD HAVE ACED THE PRESENTATION IF SHE HADN'T BEEN DEPENDING ON ME TO DO ALL THE TALKING.

IT'S A SHAME WILLOW DOUBTS HERSELF AND CLAMS UP LIKE THAT. SHE'S SO SMART AND FUN WHEN SHE OPENS UP.

I KNOW.

I WISH I COULD PROVE TO HER THAT SHE CAN DO THIS SCOUT STUFF ON HER OWN.

HMMM...

HEY—OH, SORRY, DIDN'T KNOW YOU WERE ON VIDEO.

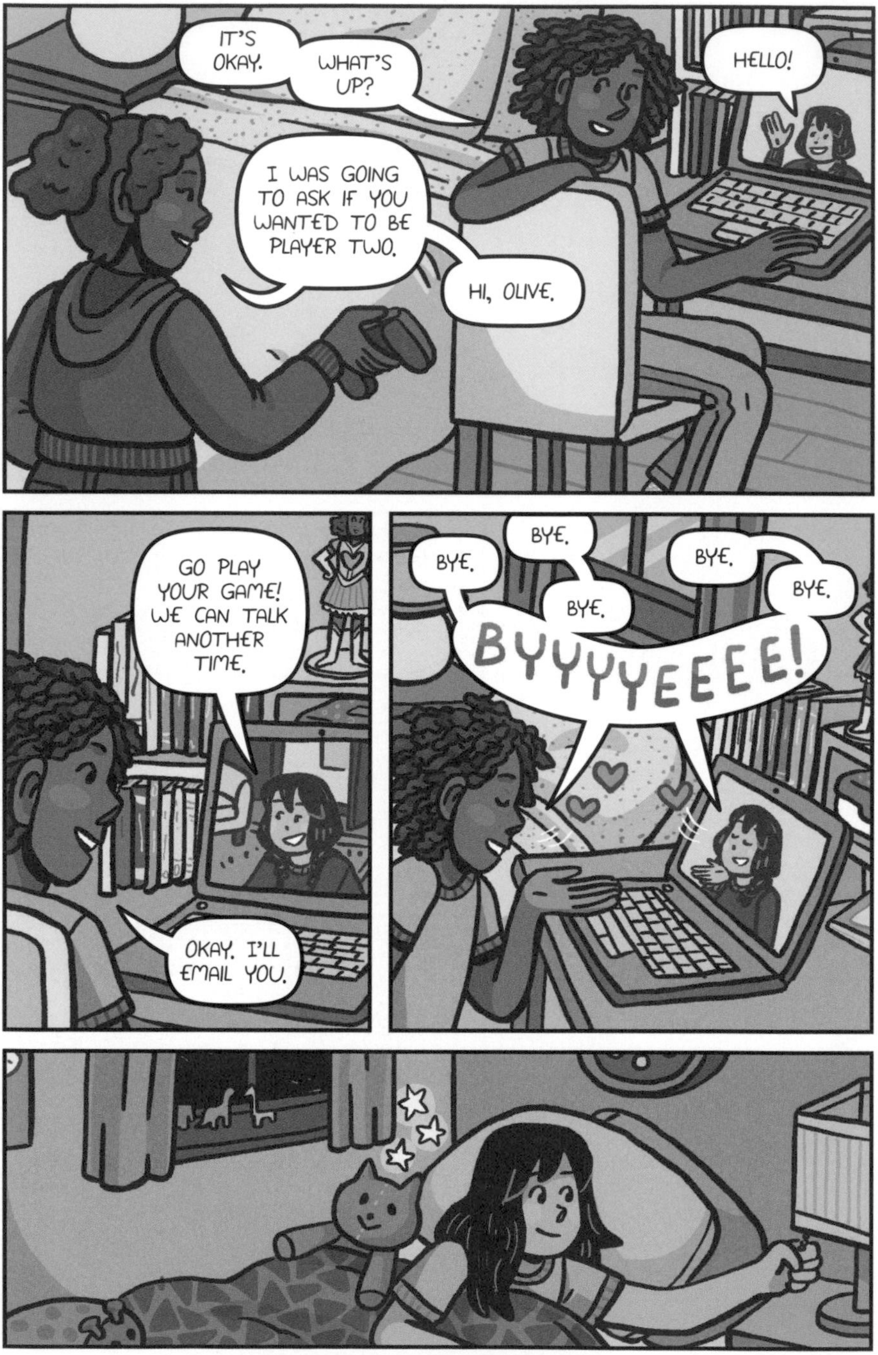

IT'S OKAY.
WHAT'S UP?
HELLO!
I WAS GOING TO ASK IF YOU WANTED TO BE PLAYER TWO.
HI, OLIVE.
GO PLAY YOUR GAME! WE CAN TALK ANOTHER TIME.
OKAY. I'LL EMAIL YOU.
BYE.
BYE.
BYE.
BYE.
BYE.
BYYYYEEEE!

KNOCK KNOCK

GOOD MORNING!

HEY, AUNT MOLLY!

ARE YOU SURE YOU WANT TO COME TO WORK WITH ME TODAY, SUGAR?

YOU WON'T GET A PAYCHECK.

YOU COULD ALWAYS PUT YOUR JAMMIES BACK ON AND HAVE A RELAXING MORNING INSTEAD OF SPENDING ALL DAY AT THE LIBRARY.

THAT'S WHAT I'D DO.

I NEED TO DO SOME RESEARCH—AND I WANT A PLACE WHERE I CAN WORK **UNDISTURBED** IF I'M GOING TO REWRITE MY MOVIE SCRIPT BY TOMORROW.

LET'S GO!

AT LEAST LET ME GRAB A CINNAMON ROLL FIRST!

159

WOW!

FILMMAKING, SCREENWRITING, STOP-MOTION ANIMATION...

I HOPE YOU STILL FOUND TIME TO PRACTICE YOUR GUITAR THIS WEEK.

SOFIA!

I REALLY **HAVE** BEEN PRACTICING.

BUT...

...I MIGHT NOT HAVE BEEN PRACTICING THE PIECES I WAS **SUPPOSED** TO BE PRACTICING.

GO ON.

WELL, I'M MAKING A MOVIE...

I CAN SEE THAT.

AND I FOUND A SONG ON THE INTERNET THAT I WANTED TO USE IN MY FILM, SO I'VE BEEN TRYING TO TEACH MYSELF.

YOU CAN READ THIS? IT LOOKS LIKE IT WAS ARRANGED FOR PIANO.

I KNOW, BUT I FIGURED OUT MY OWN GUITAR TABS—SEE?

OLIVE.

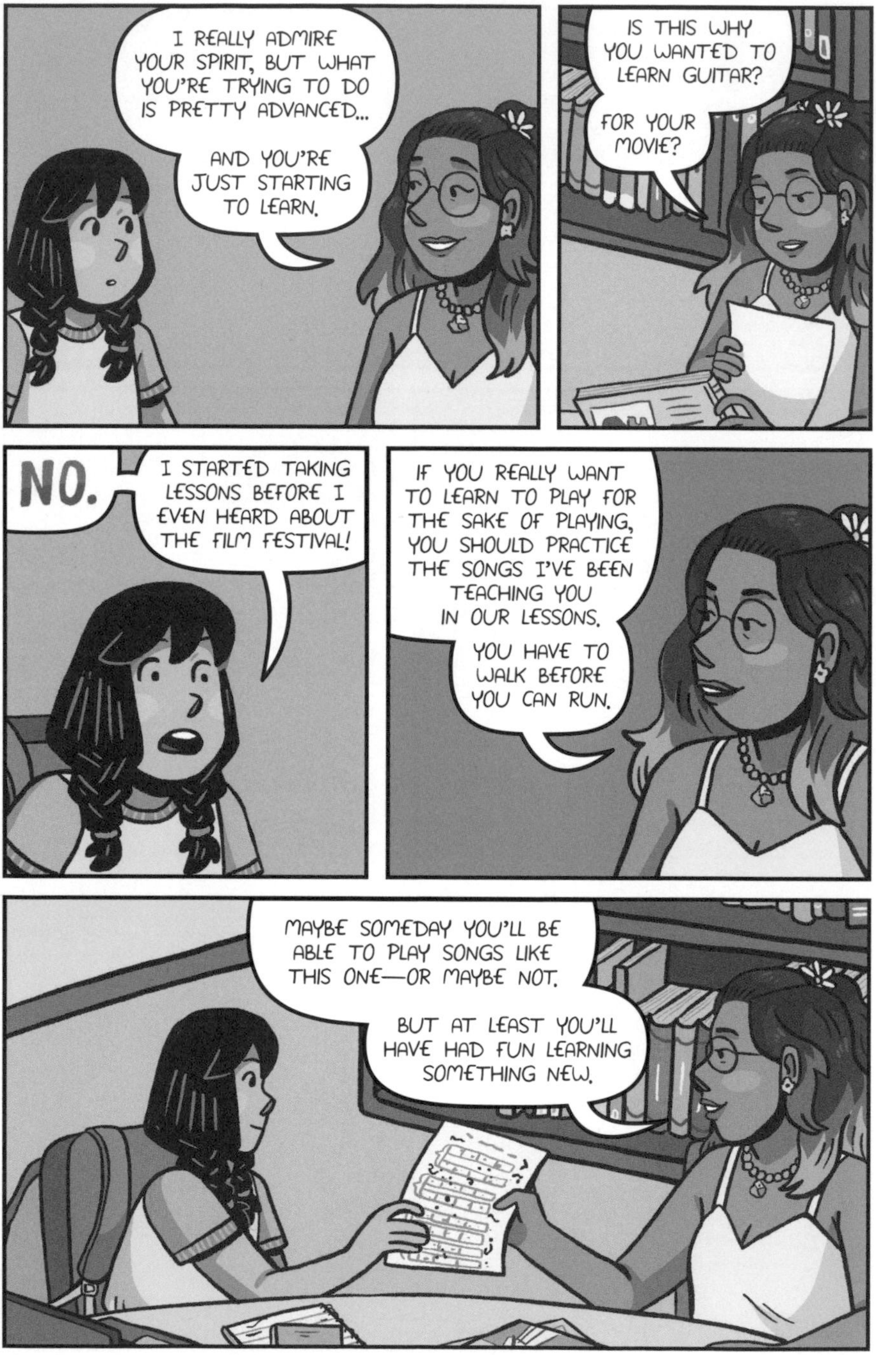
I REALLY ADMIRE YOUR SPIRIT, BUT WHAT YOU'RE TRYING TO DO IS PRETTY ADVANCED...
AND YOU'RE JUST STARTING TO LEARN.
IS THIS WHY YOU WANTED TO LEARN GUITAR?
FOR YOUR MOVIE?
NO.
I STARTED TAKING LESSONS BEFORE I EVEN HEARD ABOUT THE FILM FESTIVAL!
IF YOU REALLY WANT TO LEARN TO PLAY FOR THE SAKE OF PLAYING, YOU SHOULD PRACTICE THE SONGS I'VE BEEN TEACHING YOU IN OUR LESSONS.
YOU HAVE TO WALK BEFORE YOU CAN RUN.
MAYBE SOMEDAY YOU'LL BE ABLE TO PLAY SONGS LIKE THIS ONE—OR MAYBE NOT.
BUT AT LEAST YOU'LL HAVE HAD FUN LEARNING SOMETHING NEW.

FUN.

I HAVEN'T BEEN HAVING MUCH OF THAT LATELY.

EVERYTHING I WANT TO DO SOUNDS FUN ON ITS OWN, BUT THEN IT PILES UP...

AND I WANT TO GIVE EVERYTHING MY ALL AND DO THE BEST THAT I POSSIBLY CAN—

—BUT WHEN I DO THAT, I RUN OUT OF STEAM AND MESS THINGS UP!

AND LET PEOPLE DOWN.

I KNOW THIS STORY.

I'VE LIVED THIS STORY.

YOU'RE PASSIONATE AND ENTHUSIASTIC...AND THAT'S GOOD, BUT NO ONE CAN BURN THEIR BRIGHTEST ALL OF THE TIME—

THAT'S HOW YOU BURN **OUT**.

IT CAN BE HARD, BUT ONE OF THE MOST IMPORTANT THINGS YOU CAN LEARN TO DO IS PRIORITIZE.

THERE ARE GOING TO BE PURSUITS THAT CALL TO YOU AND MAKE YOU WANT TO WORK YOUR HARDEST EVEN WHEN IT'S DIFFICULT.

AND OTHER ACTIVITIES THAT YOU DO JUST FOR FUN—AND OTHERS THAT YOU LET GO OF ENTIRELY.

THANKS, SOFIA.

I PROBABLY NEEDED TO HEAR THAT.

ONE MORE THING YOU SHOULD HEAR: ASK FOR HELP IF YOU NEED IT.

YEAH, I'VE HEARD THAT ONE BEFORE.

THEN START **LISTENING**.

FOR EXAMPLE, IF YOU STILL NEED MUSIC FOR YOUR FILM, YOU HAPPEN TO KNOW A MODERATELY TALENTED MUSICIAN.

ARE YOU SERIOUS? THANK YOU, THANK YOU, **THANK YOU!**

JUST LET ME KNOW WHAT YOU'RE LOOKING FOR.

WHAT'S ALL OF THE COMMOTION OVER HERE?

OH!

HI, SOFIA.

HELLO.

I CAME HERE HOPING TO FIND A NEW FAVORITE BOOK, BUT INSTEAD I FOUND AN OLD FAVORITE PUPIL.

PERHAPS YOU COULD HELP ME FIND A BOOK AS WELL?

YEAH, OF COURSE! THAT **IS** MY JOB—

ER, PART OF MY JOB. YOU KNOW WHAT I MEAN.

TELL MOM I'LL CATCH A RIDE HOME WITH WILLOW.

OKAY, SUGAR. HAVE FUN AT YOUR SCOUT MEETING.

SURE.

LOOK, THERE'S OLIVE!

OLIVE!

ALL RIGHT, EVERYBERRY!

TODAY WE'RE GOING TO GO ON A NATURE HIKE TO LEARN ABOUT SOME OF THE PLANTS THAT GROW IN OUR REGION.

HERE'S A NICE LITTLE SAMPLING OF FOLIAGE.

WHO CAN TELL ME WHICH, IF ANY, OF THESE PLANTS IS HARMFUL?

WE KNOW THIS FROM SUMMER CAMP.

YOU SHOULD ANSWER!

DO YOU TWO BLUEBERRIES HAVE SOMETHING JUICY TO SHARE?

YEAH, WILLOW WANTS TO—

MMPH!

NO! WHOA!

THAT'S *POISON OAK!*

VERY GOOD, WILLOW. THAT *IS* POISON OAK, A TOXICODENDRON.

OLIVE WOULD HAVE BEEN VERY ITCHY RIGHT NOW IF YOU HADN'T CAUGHT HER.

LET'S CONTINUE... *CAREFULLY.*

NICE SAVE, WILLOW.

A TOTAL HERO MOMENT!

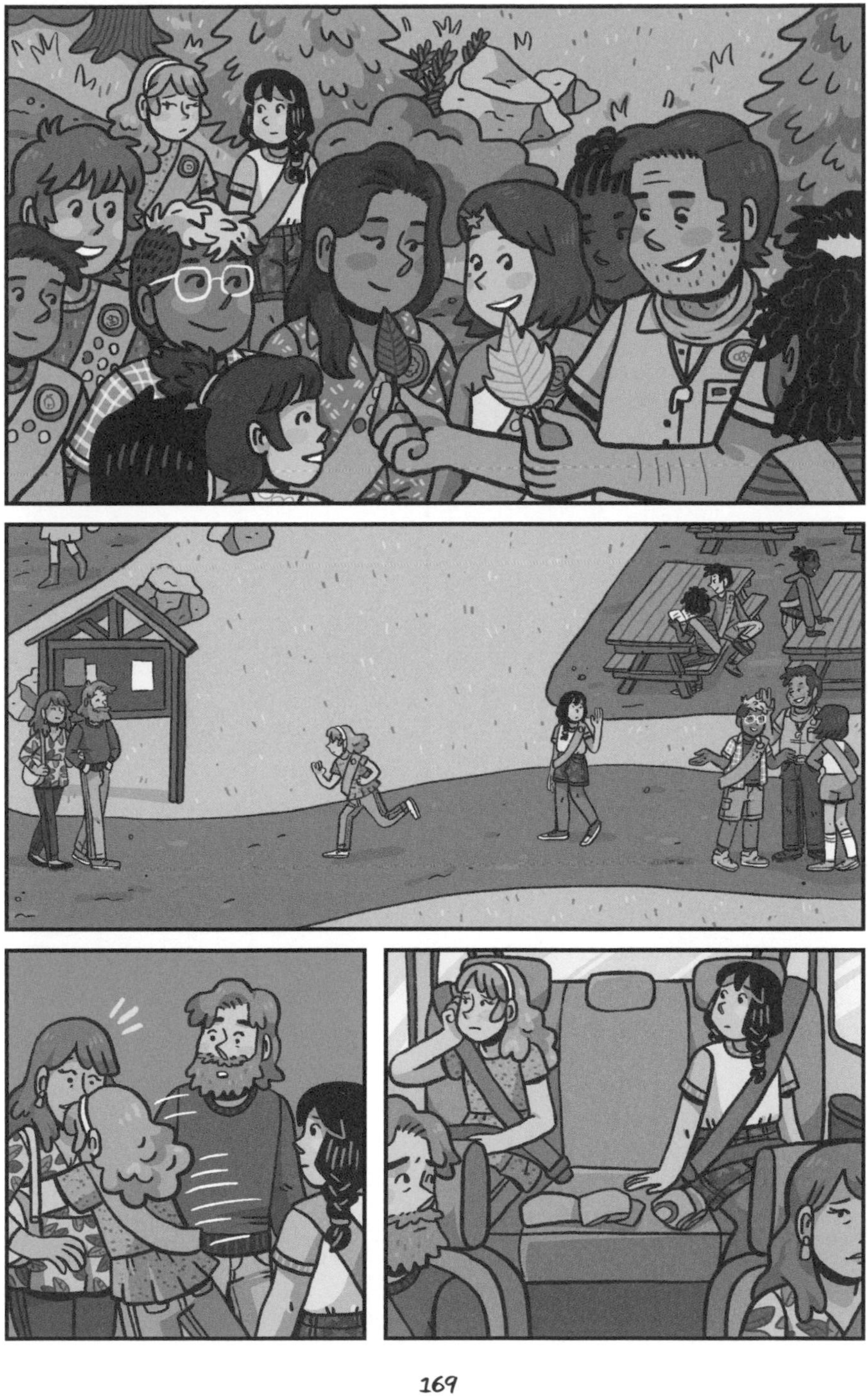

DID YOU GET BITTEN BY A ZOMBIE AT BERRY SCOUTS OR SOMETHING?

PATOOIE!

I'M JUST THINKING ABOUT WILLOW. I'M GOING TO GIVE THE MAIN CHARACTER ROLE IN THE MOVIE TO AVA, BUT I WANT WILLOW TO HAVE SOMETHING TO DO SO SHE CAN FEEL INCLUDED.

WHY DON'T YOU LET WILLOW DO SOMETHING SHE'S GOOD AT?

I THINK YOU'RE ONTO SOMETHING.

MOM!

DO WE HAVE A FIRST-AID KIT?

CLACK CLICK CLICK

WHAT'S MY MOTIVATION HERE?

I'VE ALREADY REHEARSED A LOT OF THIS, SO YOU WANT TO RUN LINES?

THAT WOULD BE GREAT!

SO THIS IS THE ZOOM...

YEAH, AND YOU CAN ROTATE THE CAMERA LIKE THIS TO PAN.

UH, HELLO?

WILLOW! HEY!

DID YOU STILL NEED MY HELP, OR...

OF COURSE! I WROTE A NEW PART **JUST FOR YOU.**

DON'T WORRY, THERE AREN'T MANY LINES.

I DON'T KNOW, OLIVE... WHAT IF I MESS IT UP?

LOOK AROUND— EVERYONE HERE IS YOUR FRIEND!

WE ALL WANT YOU TO DO WELL AND NO ONE IS JUDGING YOU.

PLUS, THERE'S PLENTY OF ROOM ON THE MEMORY CARD FOR DO-OVERS.

OKAY...

I'M READY FOR MY CLOSE-UP!

WAIT... YOU'RE REPLACING ME?

I WANT TO BE THE MONSTER!

YOU SAID I COULD! IT'S NOT MY FAULT I'M NOT SCARY!

YOU'RE **BOTH** GOING TO BE MONSTERS, OKAY?

THE NEW SCRIPT HAS A BIG-BROTHER MONSTER AND A LITTLE-BROTHER MONSTER.

I'M EXCITED TO BE MONSTER BROS WITH YOU.

MONSTER-FIVE?

RAWR!

AW, YEAH!

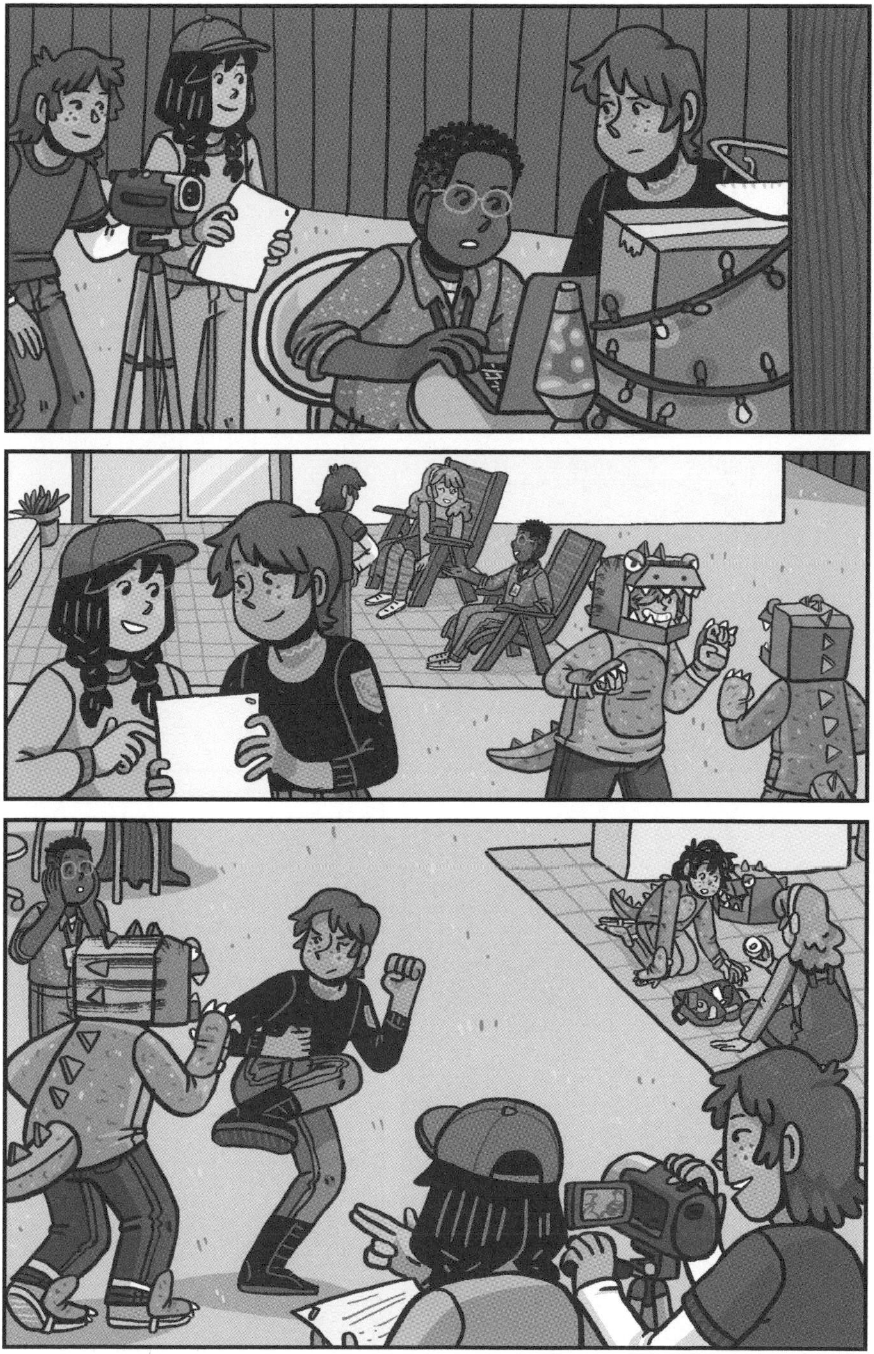

CRAFT SERVICES!

WHAT DO YOU THINK, LIV? IS THE NEW FOOTAGE LOOKING GOOD?

IT LOOKS **GREAT.**

NOW ALL YOU HAVE TO DO IS FIGURE OUT HOW TO GET THE STOP-MOTION STUFF TO LOOK GOOD.

YOU KNOW WHO YOU SHOULD TALK TO?

CHANDA! SHE'S GOOD WITH CAMERAS.

THAT'S TRUE— SHE'S ALWAYS POSTING REALLY COOL GLAMOUR SHOTS OF BETH.

JUST LOOK AT THIS PHOTO—

—I'M PRETTY SURE SHE HAS A MINI PHOTO STUDIO IN HER ROOM JUST FOR TAKING PICTURES OF HER CAT.

THAT'S A GOOD IDEA. I COULD USE ALL THE HELP I CAN GET.

HEY, GUYS!

HEY, OLIVE.

I HAVE A QUESTION FOR YOU, CHANDA...

I'M TRYING TO SHOOT A STOP-MOTION SCENE FOR A FILM I'M MAKING—

—I WAS WONDERING IF YOU COULD HELP ME OUT, SINCE YOU'RE OUR CLASS'S PHOTOGRAPHER EXTRAORDINAIRE?

I HAVE BEEN LOOKING TO DIVERSIFY MY SKILL SET.

I'LL HAVE TO CHECK WITH MY FOLKS, BUT WOULD YOU WANT TO COME OVER TOMORROW?

YEAH!

DO YOU WANT TO COME OVER TOO, BETH? WE MAY NEED AN EXTRA SET OF HANDS.

OF COURSE! WHAT ARE BESTIES FOR?

ARE YOU ACTUALLY PRACTICING BEFORE THE LAST MINUTE?

DID YOU FORGET WHAT DAY IT IS? YOUR MUSIC LESSON ISN'T UNTIL THE DAY AFTER TOMORROW.

I KNOW... BUT I WAS HOPING I COULD GO OVER TO CHANDA'S TOMORROW IF I GOT MY PRACTICING OUT OF THE WAY TODAY?

THAT'S FINE BY ME. YOUR PLAYING SOUNDS LOVELY TONIGHT, BY THE WAY.

THANKS, MOM.

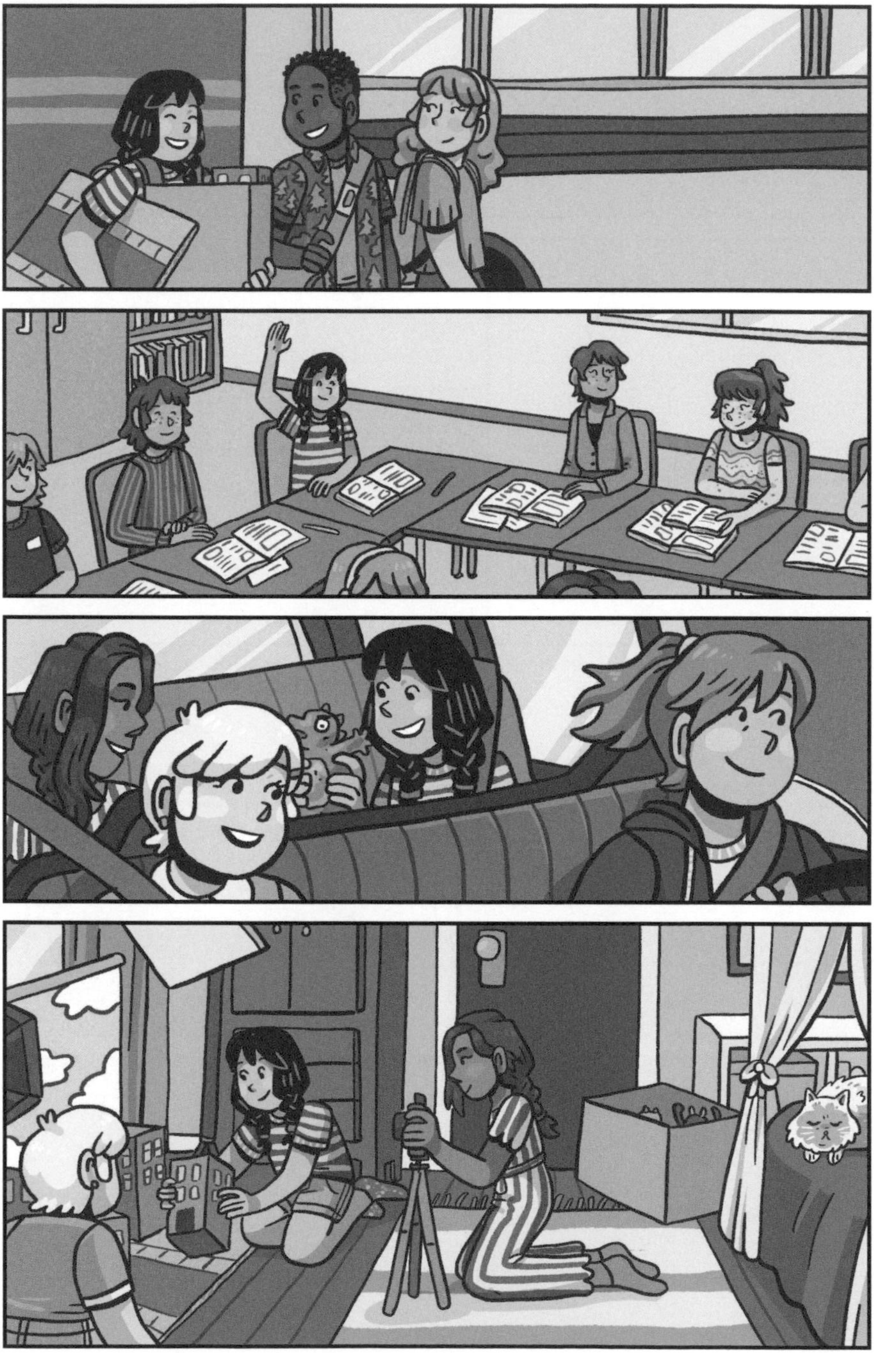

PURRRRRRR

SHE JUST CAN'T GET ENOUGH OF THE LIMELIGHT.

I'LL MOVE HER.

WAIT! THIS IS PERFECT!

I HAD TO RUSH TO MAKE ANOTHER MONSTER AFTER I REWROTE THE SCRIPT... AND THE ONE THAT I CAME UP WITH IS A LITTLE **ROUGH**.

COUNTESS PAWSBURY WOULD BE A MUCH BETTER BIG BAD, IF SHE'S UP TO IT.

WHAT DO YOU SAY, DARLING?

ARE YOU READY TO BE A MOVIE STAR?

LET'S GET HER INTO HAIR AND MAKEUP!

FLUFF!

BOOP.

BOOP.

MEOW!

I'LL SEND YOU THE ANIMATED SEQUENCE TOMORROW.

YOU MEAN YOU'LL ACTUALLY ANIMATE IT?

I FIGURED YOU'D JUST SEND ME THE PHOTOS. YOU'VE BOTH ALREADY HELPED SO MUCH.

I DON'T MIND.

I CAN DO IT IN ONE OF THE PROGRAMS I ALREADY HAVE ON MY COMPUTER.

YOU'RE THE BEST!

THANK YOU!

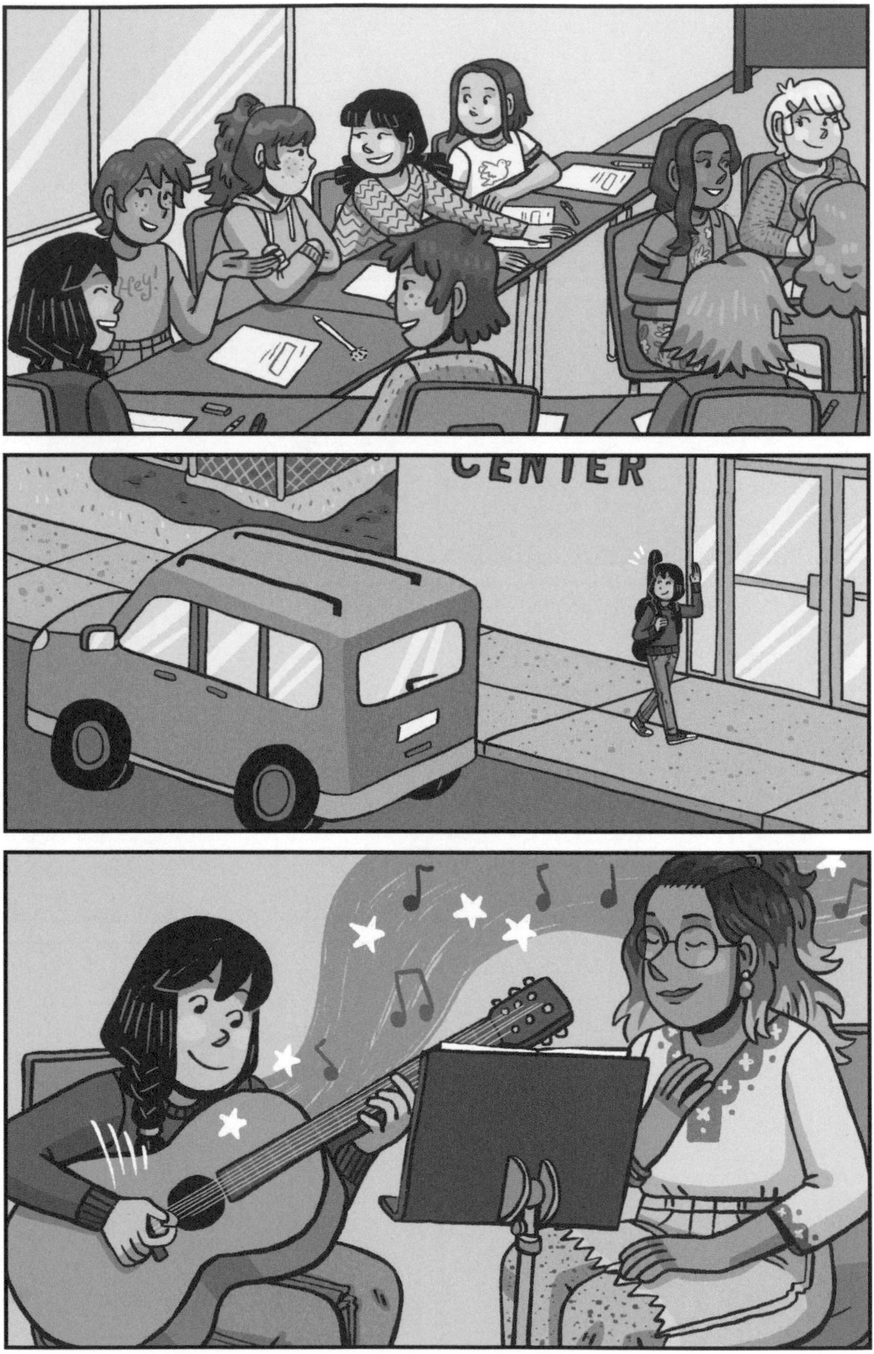
Hey!
CENTER

YOU DID VERY WELL THIS WEEK!

IF YOU KEEP THIS UP, YOU'LL BE READY TO MOVE ON TO THE NEXT SET OF SONGS I WANT TO TEACH YOU IN NO TIME.

AND HERE'S THE MUSIC I PROMISED. I HOPE THE SONGS WORK WELL WITH YOUR FOOTAGE.

THANKS, SOFIA! YOU'RE A LIFESAVER.

THE MOVIE HAS TO BE SUBMITTED TONIGHT IF I WANT IT TO GET INTO THE FILM FESTIVAL, SO I HAVE MY WORK CUT OUT FOR ME!

WAIT!

YOU'RE GOING TO COME TO THE FILM FESTIVAL, RIGHT?

I WOULDN'T MISS IT.

IS THE MOVIE DONE? CAN I SEE?

GET OUT OF HERE! YOU CAN SEE IT AT THE PREMIERE LIKE EVERYONE ELSE.

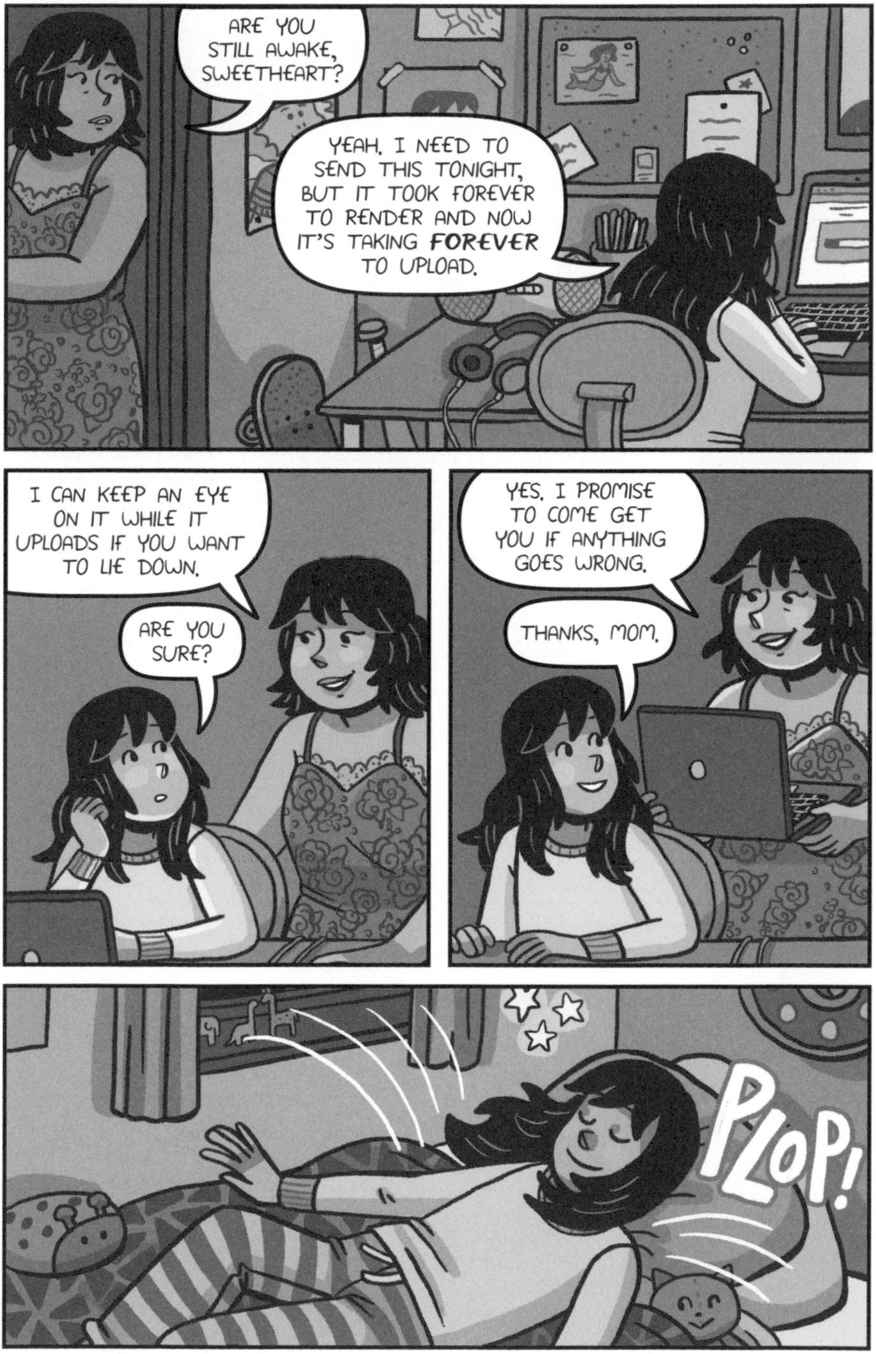
ARE YOU STILL AWAKE, SWEETHEART?
YEAH. I NEED TO SEND THIS TONIGHT, BUT IT TOOK FOREVER TO RENDER AND NOW IT'S TAKING **FOREVER** TO UPLOAD.
I CAN KEEP AN EYE ON IT WHILE IT UPLOADS IF YOU WANT TO LIE DOWN.
ARE YOU SURE?
YES. I PROMISE TO COME GET YOU IF ANYTHING GOES WRONG.
THANKS, MOM.
PLOP!

MOM, DID—

YES, YOUR FILM IS OFFICIALLY UPLOADED AND SUBMITTED.

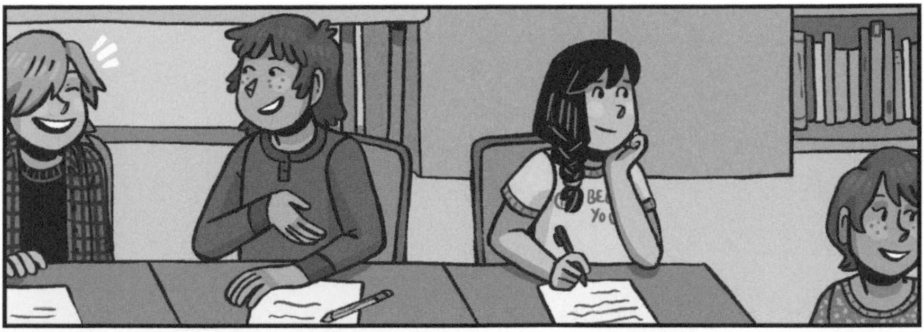
BE
YOU

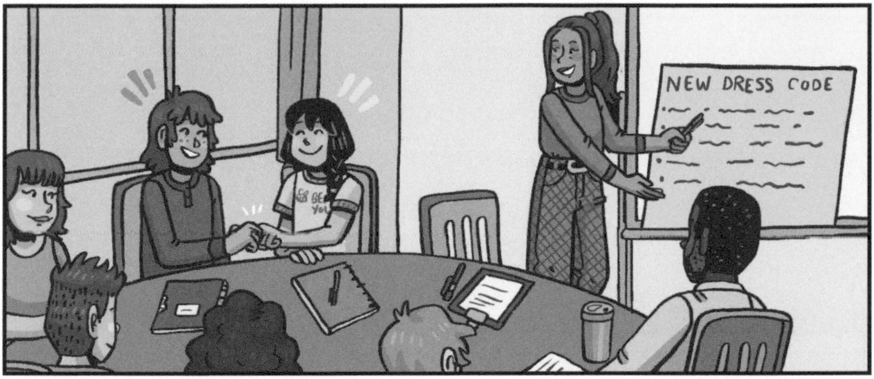
NEW DRESS CODE

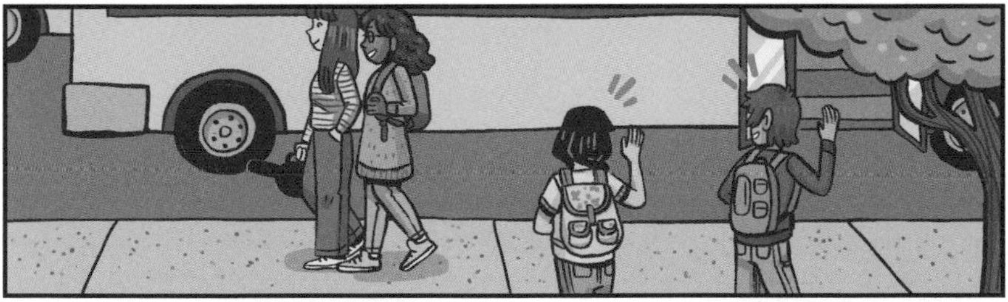

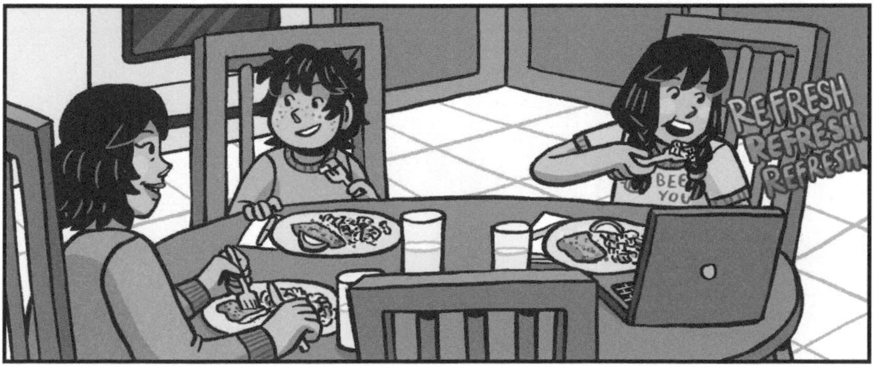
REFRESH
REFRESH
REFRESH
BEE
YOU

REFRESH
REFRESH
REFRESH

REFRESH
REFRESH
REFRESH

REFRESH
REFRESH
REFRESH

BEEP!

EW MAIL!

HAS OLIVE FINALLY LOST IT?

MAYBE. SHE'S BEEN LIKE THAT ALL MORNING.

WHAT'S UP?

THE MOVIE GOT INTO THE FILM FESTIVAL!

THAT'S RAD!

MY BIG-SCREEN DEBUT!

CAN WE ALL GO SEE IT?

CONGRATS!

DOES THIS MEAN PEOPLE ARE ACTUALLY GOING TO *SEE* ME ACT?

IT'S JUST A LOCAL THING, RIGHT?

YEAH. AND ANYWAY, ALL THEY'RE GOING TO SEE IS HOW AMAZING YOU DID!

BEEP
BEEP

WOW, WILLOW, THAT LOOKS GREAT. COULD YOU PAINT A DAISY ON MINE?

UM, OKAY.

DAD! LOOK!

ELDERBERRY TODD, CAN I TALK TO YOU FOR A SECOND?

SURE— WHAT'S ON YOUR MIND?

I THINK THIS MIGHT BE MY LAST MEETING.

IS EVERYTHING OKAY?

YEAH— I JUST DON'T THINK I'M A BERRY SCOUT.

I GAVE IT A TRY, BUT IT'S NOT FOR ME.

THAT'S FAIR.

IT'S NOT FOR EVERYBERRY.

I KNOW THAT IT'S KIND OF A BIG ASK, CONSIDERING I JUST QUIT...

...BUT WILLOW AND I MADE A MOVIE THAT'S GOING TO PLAY AT A FILM FESTIVAL AT THE COMMUNITY CENTER TOMORROW.

IT WOULD MEAN A LOT TO ME—AND WILLOW— IF YOU COULD COME WATCH IT.

FILM FESTIVAL

YOU AND WILLOW MADE A MOVIE?

CAN WE COME?

YEAH, I WANT TO SEE THAT!

OLIVE, COME ON!

YEAH!

EVERYONE'S INVITED!

OLIVE, ARE YOU READY TO GO? WE STILL NEED TO PICK UP HUGH AND WILLOW.

YEAH, I'M COMING.

RAWR!

YOU'RE GOING TO WEAR THAT ALL NIGHT?

I WANT PEOPLE TO RECOGNIZE ME!

I'M THE STAR OF THE MOVIE, AFTER ALL.

I'VE LITERALLY CREATED A MONSTER.

OLIVE'S HERE!

COME ON, I WANT US TO GET GOOD SEATS.

THE BERRY SCOUTS?

DID YOU KNOW THE BERRY SCOUTS WOULD BE HERE?

YEAH— I INVITED THEM.

LISTEN, WILLOW, WE NEED TO TALK—

ALL RIGHT! IT'S TIME TO ROCK AND ROLL!

WE HAVE A LOT OF AWESOME FILMS TONIGHT FROM CREATORS OF ALL AGES, SO LET'S GET STARTED!

WE'LL TALK LATER.

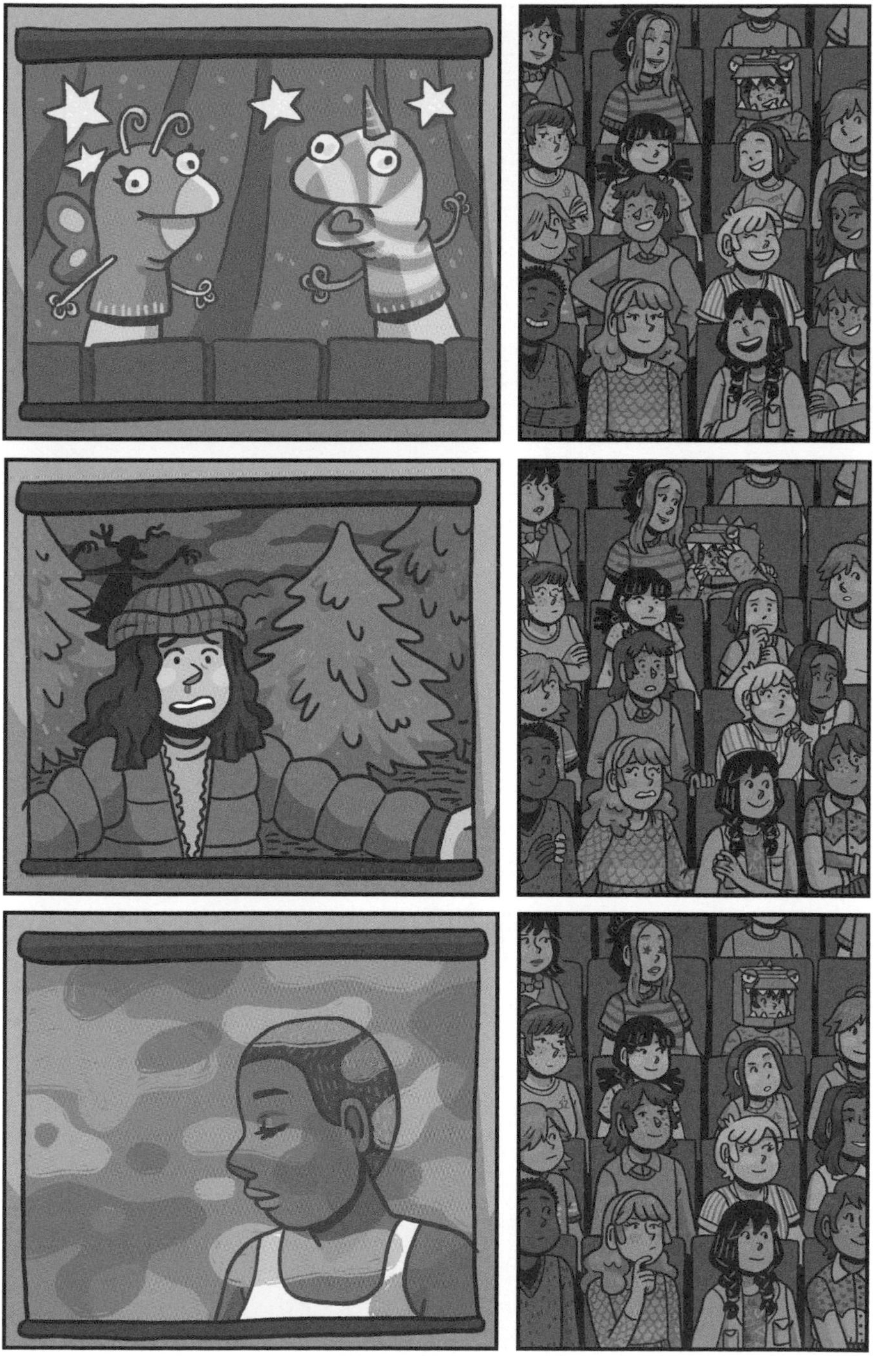

OLIVE BRANCHE'S
3 MONSTERS

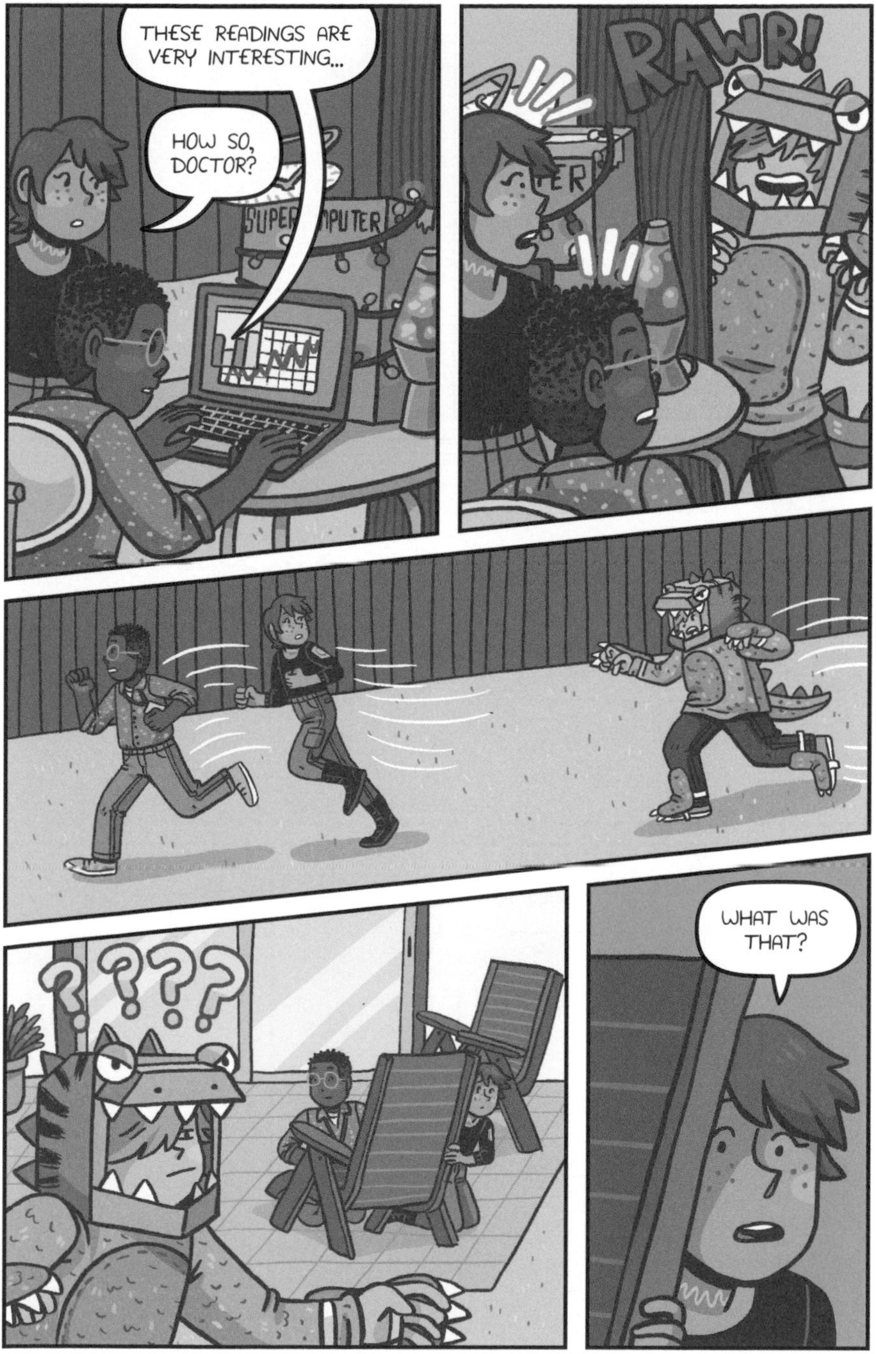
THESE READINGS ARE VERY INTERESTING...
HOW SO, DOCTOR?
SUPER COMPUTER
RAWR!
WHAT WAS THAT?

THAT... WAS A **MONSTER**.

THE VOLCANO MUST HAVE WOKEN IT UP.

WHEN I TOOK THIS SECURITY-GUARD JOB ON MONSTER VOLCANO ISLAND,

NO ONE TOLD ME THERE'D BE **MONSTERS**.

WHY DID YOU THINK IT WAS CALLED "MONSTER VOLCANO ISLAND"?

I THOUGHT IT WAS REFERRING TO THE SIZE OF THE VOLCANO!

HMM...I GUESS WE COULD HAVE CALLED IT MONSTER **AND** VOLCANO ISLAND.

WELL, DON'T WORRY ABOUT THAT NOW, DOCTOR.

IT'S MY JOB TO PROTECT THE PEOPLE OF THIS ISLAND,

SO THAT'S WHAT I'M GOING TO DO.

HA!

GRRRRRR!

STOP FIGHTING FOR A SECOND AND LOOK!

AN EVEN BIGGER MONSTER!

THE VOLCANO MUST HAVE WOKEN HER UP, TOO!

GRR! GRR! BABA BRUBBA!

WHAT ARE YOU TRYING TO TELL ME?

BABA BRUBBA! BABA BRUBBA!

HELP! HELP!

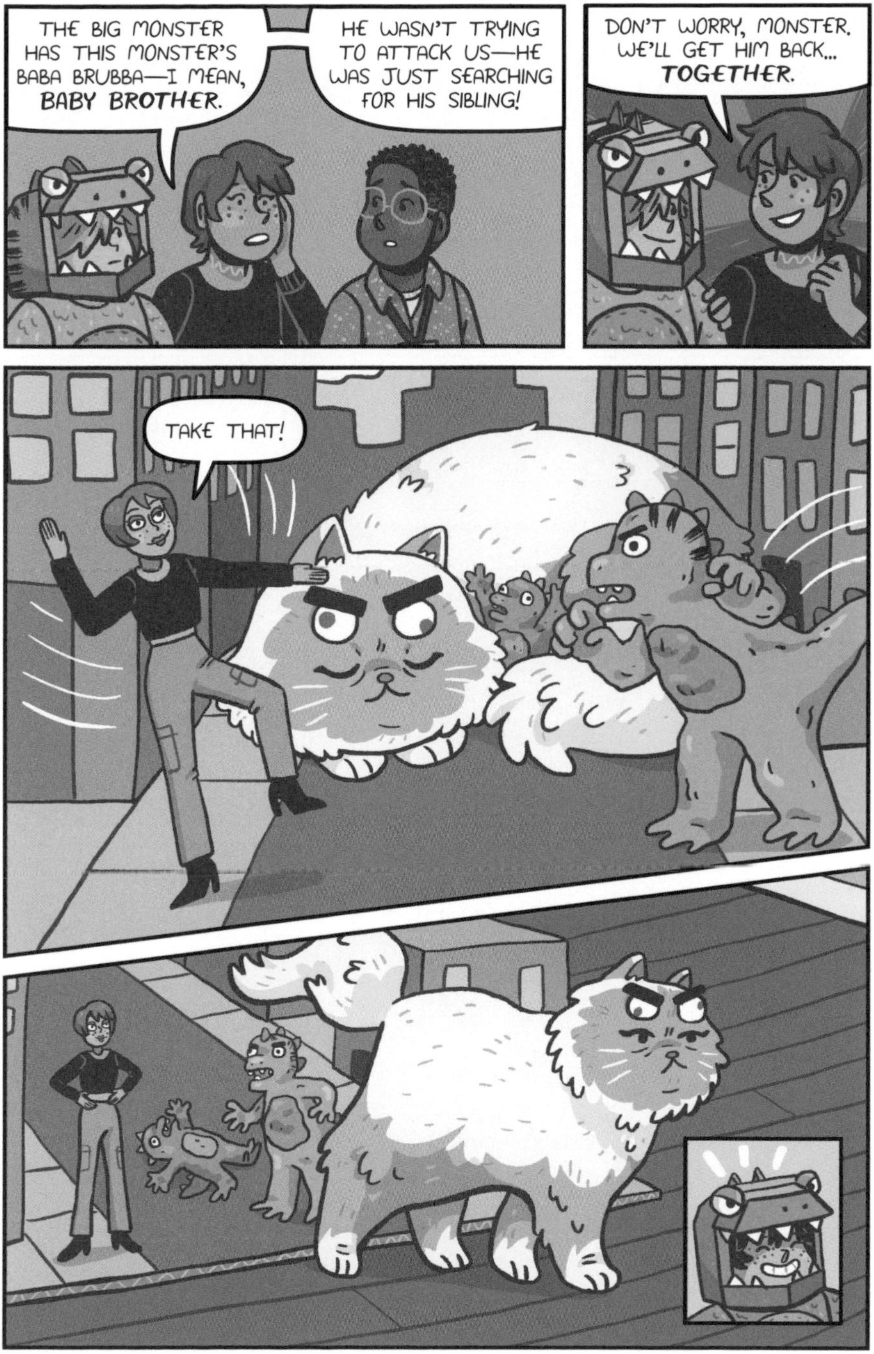
THE BIG MONSTER HAS THIS MONSTER'S BABA BRUBBA—I MEAN, **BABY BROTHER**.
HE WASN'T TRYING TO ATTACK US—HE WAS JUST SEARCHING FOR HIS SIBLING!
DON'T WORRY, MONSTER. WE'LL GET HIM BACK... **TOGETHER**.
TAKE THAT!

HE WAS HURT IN BATTLE. YOU HAVE TO HELP HIM, DOCTOR!

OOOOO!

I HAVE A DOCTORATE IN MONSTEROLOGY—

I'M NOT A MEDICAL DOCTOR!

UHH... I AM.

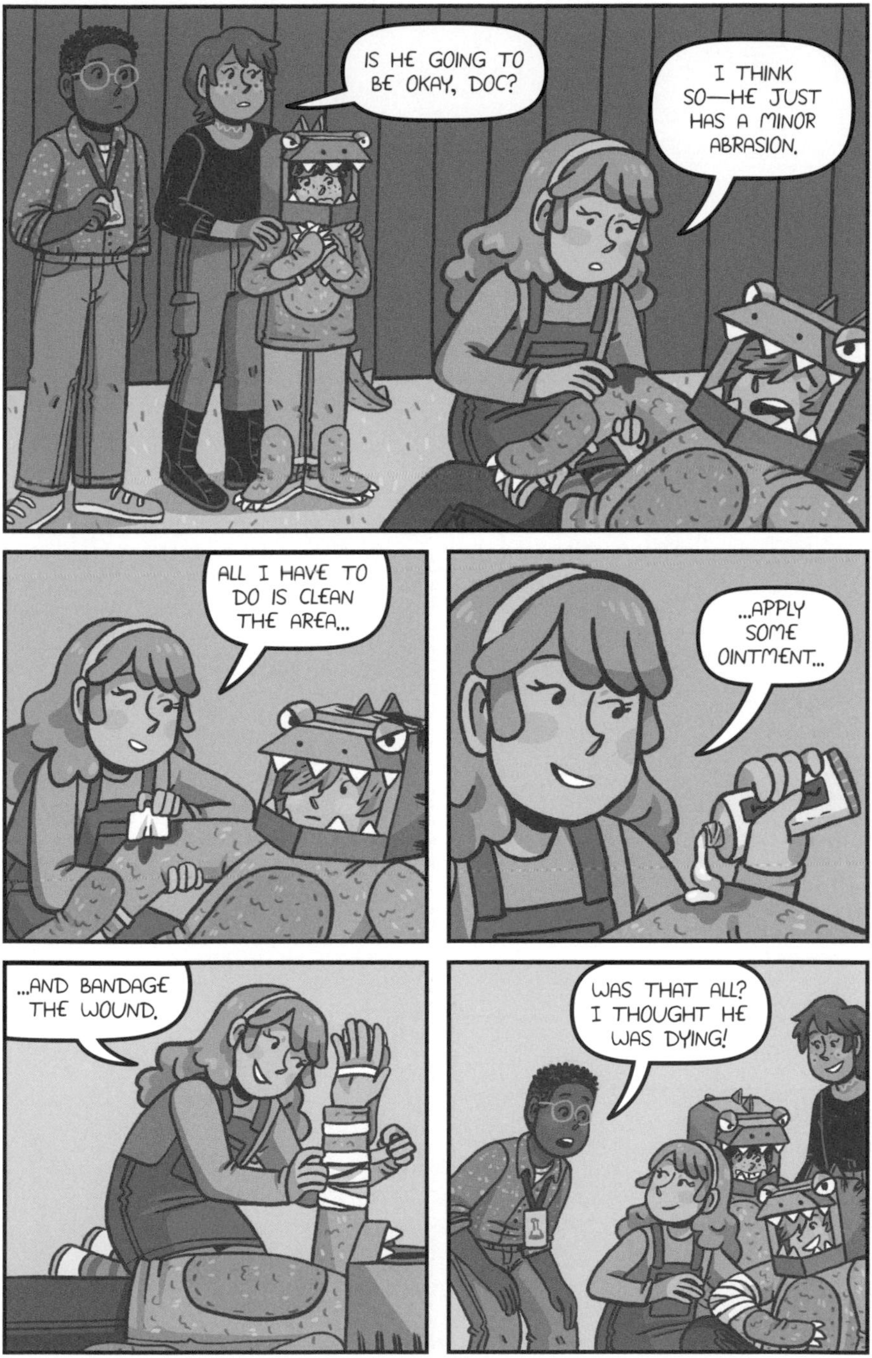
IS HE GOING TO BE OKAY, DOC?
I THINK SO—HE JUST HAS A MINOR ABRASION.
ALL I HAVE TO DO IS CLEAN THE AREA...
...APPLY SOME OINTMENT...
...AND BANDAGE THE WOUND.
WAS THAT ALL? I THOUGHT HE WAS DYING!

WRITTEN AND DIRECTED BY
OLIVE BRANCHE
STARRING
AVA CRUZ AS THE GUARD
SAWYER MOORE AS THE MONSTER
HUGH DAVIS AS THE DOCTOR
WILLOW VOSS AS THE MEDICAL DOCTOR
WITH
SIMON "GOOBER" BRANCHE AS
THE BABY MONSTER
AND
COUNTESS PAWSBURY AS
THE BIGGER MONSTER
CAMERA—**TRENT PHAN**
STOP-MOTION ANIMATION—**CHANDA BASU**
& **BETH WAGNER**
SPECIAL EFFECTS—**BREE ONAI**
MUSIC—**SOFIA RAMOS**

SPECIAL THANKS TO **LUCY BRANCHE**
AND **MOLLY AMATO**

THAT WAS SO COOL!

TOP-NOTCH EMERGENCY TREATMENT, DOCTOR WILLOW. I MIGHT HAVE TO MAKE AN EXCEPTION AND LET YOU RETAKE YOUR FIRST-AID TEST.

REALLY? THANK YOU.

OUR NEXT BADGE IS FOR NATURE SKILLS, I WAS WONDERING IF YOU'D WANT TO PARTNER UP SINCE YOU KNOW ABOUT PLANTS AND STUFF?

AND SINCE OLIVE QUIT.

THAT'S THE THING I WANTED TO "TALK LATER" ABOUT.

I THINK I SAW THIS COMING, BUT IT'S OKAY, I'VE ACTUALLY STARTED TO—

I CAN'T BELIEVE YOU WERE IN A MOVIE!

YOU'RE USUALLY SO QUIET—

WHO KNEW YOU WERE SECRETLY A MOVIE STAR!

WHAT DID YOU USE FOR MONSTER BLOOD? WAS IT GROSS?

IT WAS JUST KETCHUP.

YOU'RE OLIVE BRANCHE, RIGHT?

210

I'M SKYLER, ONE OF THE ORGANIZERS OF THE FILM FESTIVAL.

I'M REALLY IMPRESSED WITH YOUR WORK.

THANK YOU!

I'M GOING TO BE RUNNING A YOUTH FILMMAKING WORKSHOP THROUGH THE COMMUNITY CENTER STARTING NEXT MONTH. I THINK YOU'D BE A GREAT FIT FOR THE PROGRAM!

hmmm...

THANK YOU... BUT I'M GOING TO HAVE TO PASS.

I'M REALLY GLAD THAT I MADE A MOVIE FOR THE FESTIVAL AND THAT PEOPLE LIKED IT, BUT IT WAS A LOT OF WORK AND A **LOT** OF STRESS.

I'M NOT SURE I'M READY FOR ALL THAT AGAIN.

IT'D ONLY BE TWO DAYS A WEEK—

SORRY, BUT I HAVE SOME OTHER STUFF I WANT TO FOCUS ON RIGHT NOW.

ALL RIGHT, YOU DO YOU, I GUESS.

SOFIA!

WHAT A WONDERFUL FILM... I THINK THE MUSIC WAS MY FAVORITE PART.

THERE'S MY LITTLE DIRECTOR.

WE'RE GOING OUT FOR DINNER TO CELEBRATE OLIVE'S SMASH HIT—

—AND MY BREAKOUT PERFORMANCE!

WANNA COME?

I'M SO GLAD EVERYONE COULD COME OUT TONIGHT—

—BUT I HOPE WE WRAP UP SOON, I'VE GOT ONE LAST APPOINTMENT I CAN'T MISS...

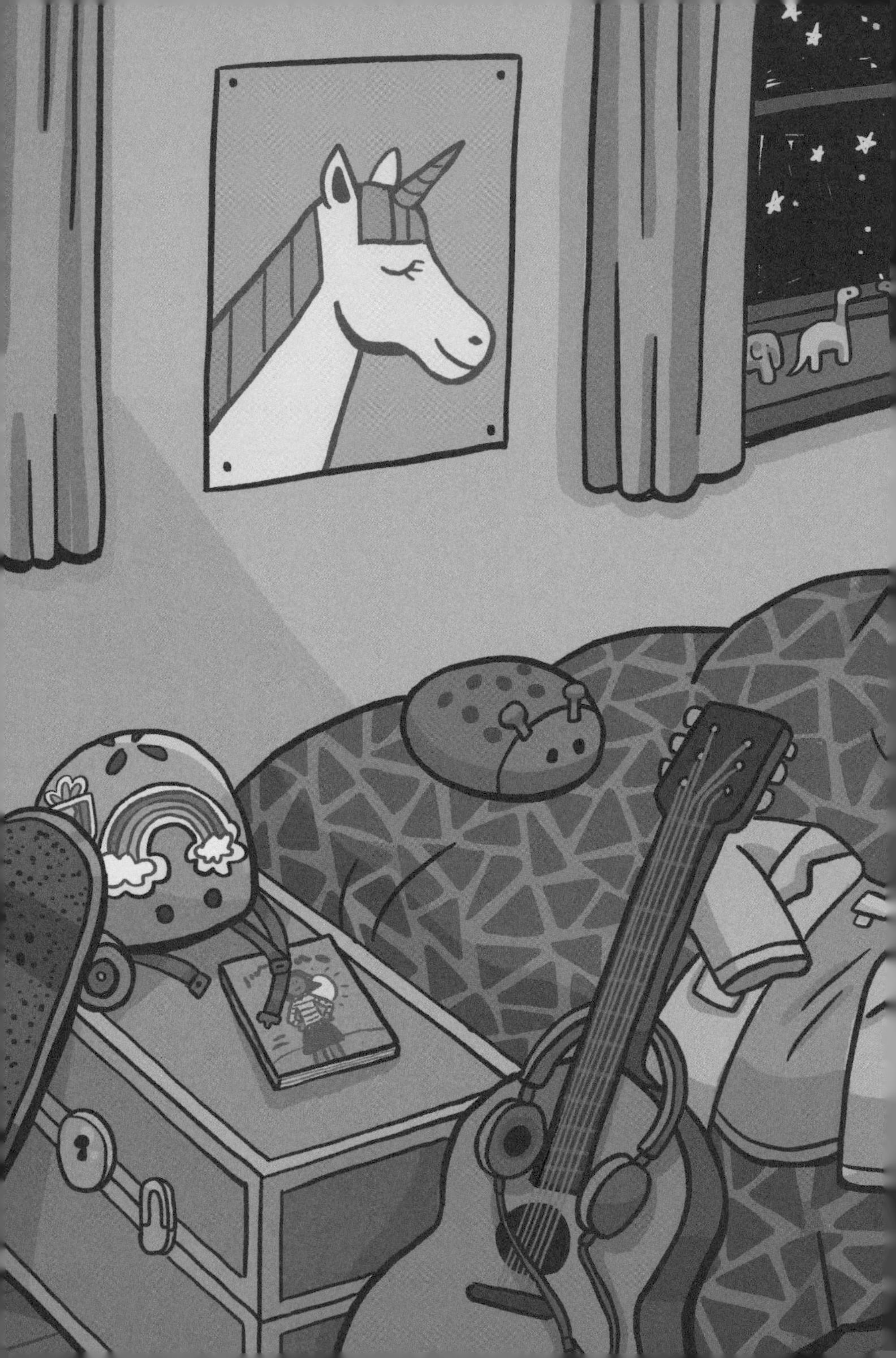

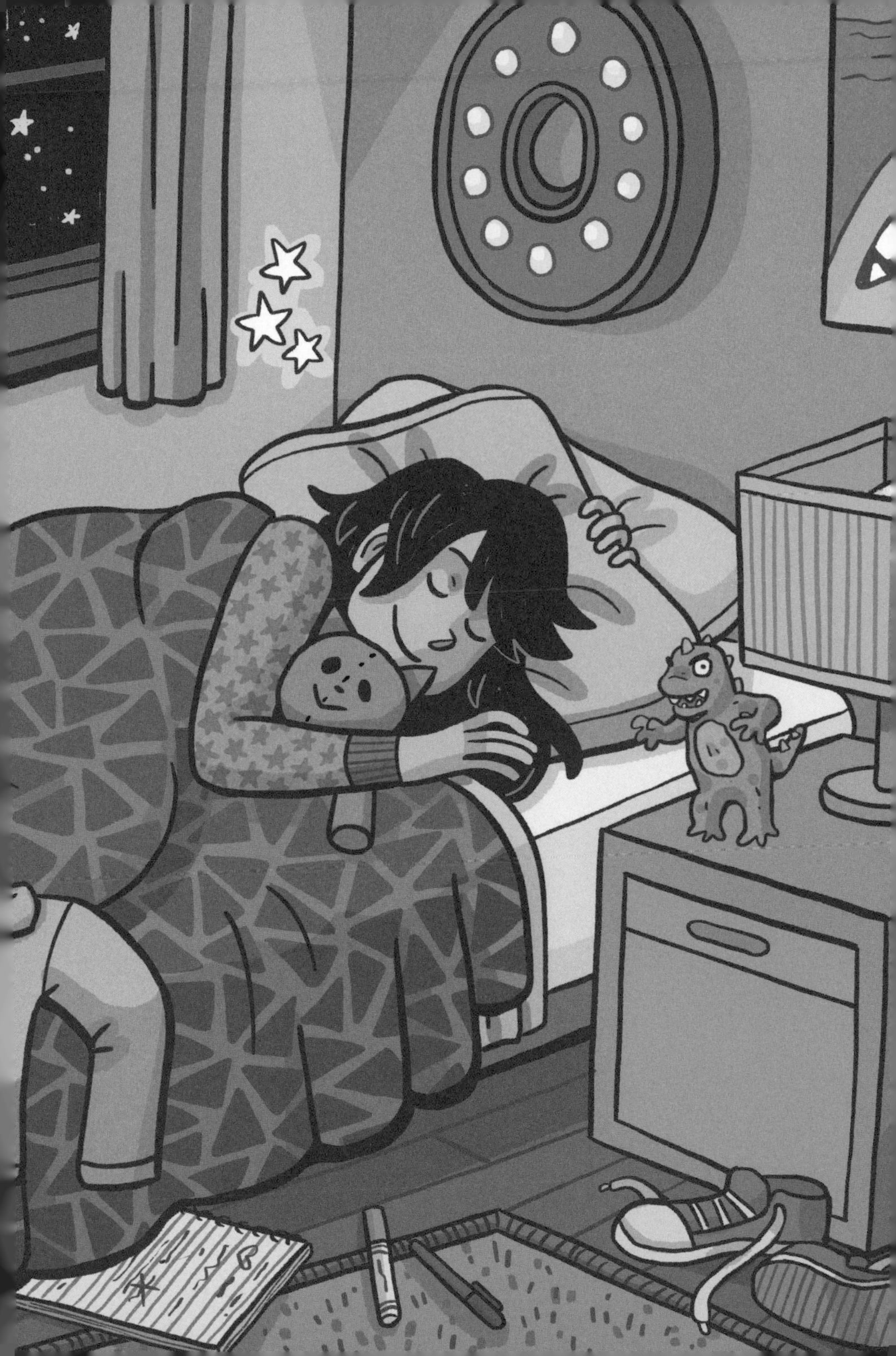

HOW "TO DO" A TO-DO LIST

When you've got a lot to do, it can feel overwhelming—but being organized can help! Here are some To-Do List tips on how to avoid the crunch and stay cool when things get busy.

Figure out your top priorities . . . and put them at the top of your list! If you take care of the most important things first, the rest of your list will feel like a breeze!

Celebrate your accomplishments! You don't need to have a dance party every time you get something done (though you totally could), but acknowledging your hard work in some way is a must. This can be as simple as marking your finished tasks with stickers.

Break big tasks down into smaller steps. Big projects like cleaning your whole room (or writing and illustrating a whole book) might seem intimidating, but breaking them down into smaller tasks can make it more manageable. This also lets you pace yourself and tackle each step in your own time.

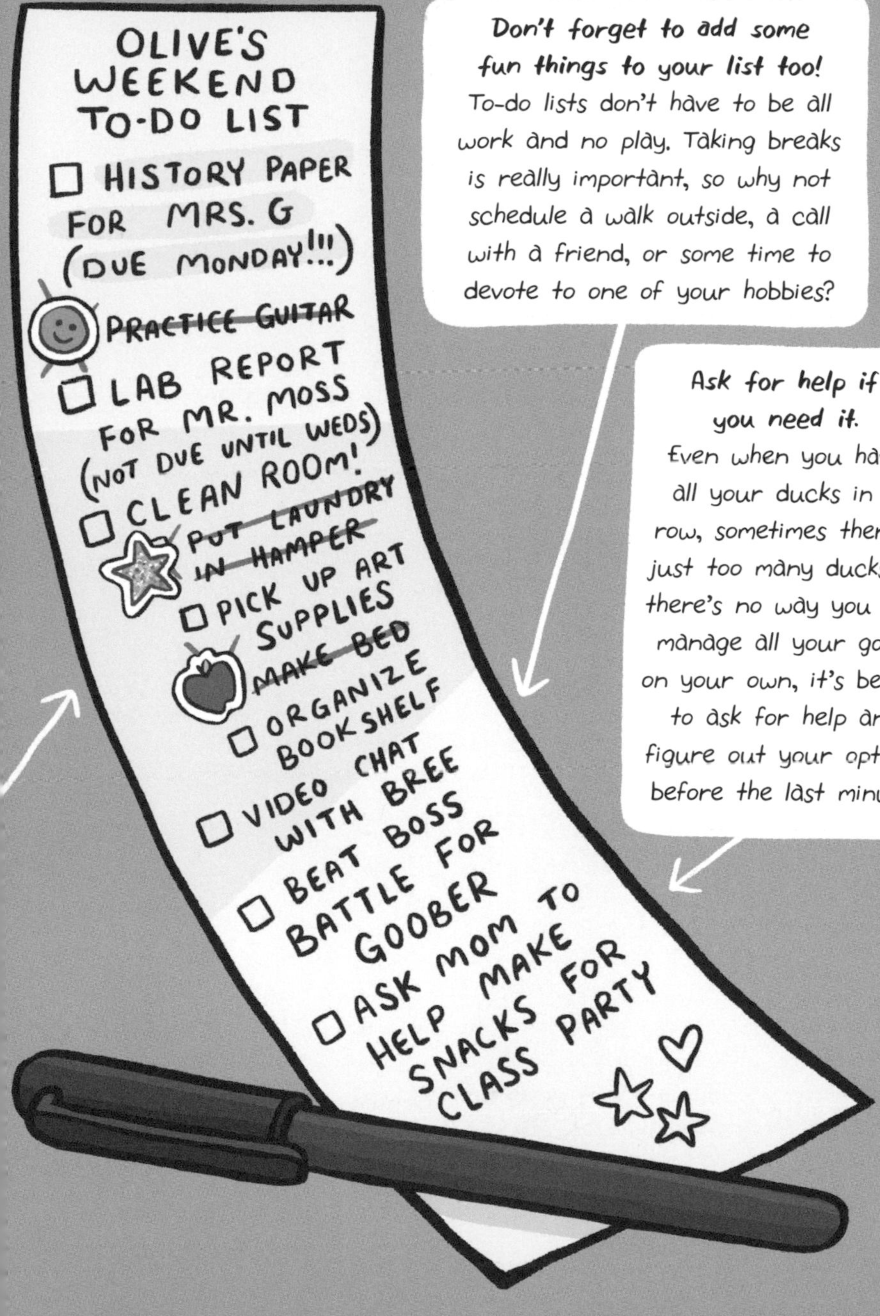
OLIVE'S WEEKEND TO-DO LIST
HISTORY PAPER FOR MRS. G (DUE MONDAY!!!)
PRACTICE GUITAR
LAB REPORT FOR MR. MOSS (NOT DUE UNTIL WEDS)
CLEAN ROOM!
PUT LAUNDRY IN HAMPER
PICK UP ART SUPPLIES
MAKE BED
ORGANIZE BOOKSHELF
VIDEO CHAT WITH BREE
BEAT BOSS BATTLE FOR GOOBER
ASK MOM TO HELP MAKE SNACKS FOR CLASS PARTY

Don't forget to add some fun things to your list too! To-do lists don't have to be all work and no play. Taking breaks is really important, so why not schedule a walk outside, a call with a friend, or some time to devote to one of your hobbies?

Ask for help if you need it. Even when you have all your ducks in a row, sometimes there's just too many ducks! If there's no way you can manage all your goals on your own, it's better to ask for help and figure out your options before the last minute.

What Is Stop-Motion Animation?

Stop motion is an animation technique that uses a series of photographs in which the subject has been moved slightly between each image to create the illusion of movement when the images are shown in succession at a high speed. Technically, all film and animation is a series of still images, but stop-motion animation allows artists to use this fact to their advantage and create footage where inanimate objects appear to be moving on their own, or beings seem able to do things that they wouldn't normally be able to do—such as making someone look like they're hovering by taking multiple pictures of them mid-jump. Stop motion has been used throughout film history in a myriad of ways, and the limits of the technique are defined only by an individual's imagination . . . and the available time and resources.

The method can be done with clay, posable puppets, paper, people, found objects, or any subject that can be arranged and photographed. The number of photos needed to create this effect varies, as does the number of images in other forms of video, but the most common for TV and film is 24 FPS (frames per second). This means that there are 24 images in each second of video! So a minute of animation at 24 FPS contains 1440 pictures. A lot of animation is "shot on twos," which means each image is shown for two frames, so there are 12 frames per second. Some animation is shot on threes or fours, but even at that lower frame rate, the animators still need to create hundreds of images for one minute of animation—and a whole lot more for an entire movie or show!

This might sound pretty complicated, but you can still make your own simple stop-motion animation at home just like Chanda, Beth, and Olive did! All you need to do is set up a camera in a way so that it won't move between pictures—a tripod works best, but if you're using a phone or tablet, a stand will work. Then, start taking photos of something! Whatever you choose as your subject, move it just a tiny little bit between each picture. The smaller the changes between each frame, the more fluid the movements will look in the finished animation. Once you have all of your images, turn them into video using a video-editing software. There are free apps for this, and some computers even come with programs already installed. Just ask a tech-savvy adult to help you get set up.

Acknowledgments

I want to express my appreciation for everyone on Team Click whose hard work helped another story exit my head and become a book! Thanks to my editor, Mary, and my agent, Elizabeth, for their continued enthusiasm for Olive and her friends. Thank you to Jess for another round of coloring, collaboration, and companionship. Thanks to Steph for designing with an attention to detail and for being so dedicated to smoothing out all the wrinkles along the way. And thank you to Lor for lending their lettering skills to the project and helping these chatty kids speak up. It's a pleasure to work with all of you!

I'd also like to extend gratitude to my friends and family for their support. As the people in my life know, Olive's struggles in this book are not unfamiliar to me, and it's nice to have loved ones who check in and make sure I don't Crunch too hard. Mom, Dad, Grandpa, Karen, Will, Kristina, Gabe, and Lish—thank you for being there for me. Special thanks to K and Tyler for sharing your animation expertise; I'm lucky to have such smart and talented pals. And lastly, Jeffrey...I'm so happy to have you by my side in life—and quite literally by my side when writing so I can ask you how to spell things.

—KAYLA

Read the *New York Times* bestselling series from
Kayla Miller

And keep the fun going with the Click companion series **Besties**, illustrated by Kristina Luu and cowritten with Jeffrey Canino!